Part I

Susan, the mice and the men

The Sexual Compass

Michael Reed

The Sexual Compass

ISBN 978-0-9560813-4-6

First edition printed 2014

Michael Reed asserts the moral right to be identified as the author of this work

© Michael Reed 2014

Unmusic Books www.unmusic.co.uk

Proofreading by Darryl Sloan darrylsloan.wordpress.com

About the author

Michael Reed is a freelance writer specialising in technology, gender politics and geek culture. He has written articles for magazines and websites such as RetroGamer, Linux User & Developer, Men's News Daily, Micro Mart, A Voice for Men, Den of Geek, Linux Journal, OSNews, OpenDemocracy and others.

Contact

www.unmusic.co.uk
mike@unmusic.co.uk

Chapter 1

Coffee, mice and sex

I'm going to tell you what happened when I first I heard about the mice. At that time, I was twenty-one years old and juggling single motherhood with studying for a degree. That morning, I had woken up early, a trade-off to have a few minutes with coffee before bedlam began. I had to make as little noise as possible to avoid waking Mum and Dad. To toe the line is a way of life when you live at home in your twenties.

I twirled down the volume of the radio before switching it on. I filled the kettle and quietly stirred the coffee, still operating like a maternal version of the Terminator following its program. Speaking of quietness, I would have thought it was still too quiet and cold for sex, particularly from the BBC, but sex was the subject at hand this morning.

The newsreader informed me: "Scientists in Manchester have announced that levels of insulin may regulate sexual orientation."

Initially, some scientists had made this discovery in mice, and now, some other scientists had confirmed it in human beings. This breakthrough was exciting news, for mice and for humans, but I risked moving away from the radio to switch the central heating on. When I returned to my seat, the newsreader had moved on to another subject, the mice and their sexual orientation be damned. It was funny, as I always felt mousy when scurrying around in the morning.

Once the heating came on, the familiar knocks and bumps from upstairs began, and my day, proper, started. Fortunately, we lived in a house big enough to have two bathrooms. As usual, I took over the upstairs bathroom to get me and Tom washed while Mum and dad got themselves into gear downstairs. Tom had reached the stage where he could wash his own face and brush his teeth while I was in the shower. Mum would have breakfast set up by the time I got downstairs. We all ate breakfast together, something I had tried to avoid when I was a teenager.

My mornings, along with my life in general, did not exhibit a great deal of variety. Following breakfast, I'd say goodbye to Mum and Dad and do the nursery run. Typically, I'd then do a shopping run and return to the empty house for lunch and then coursework. At 3pm, I'd make the return trip to pick up Tom. By the time I got back to the house, Mum would be well on with the dinner, which was always a family meal. Mum and Dad would chat away while I fed Tom. After dinner, Dad would say, "Let's see what rubbish is on," and disappear into the lounge while me and Mum would start loading up the dish washer and clearing up in general. We'd talk about nothing in particular; the trick was to avoid any deep conversation. Disagreements are potentially deadly in such a confined environment. Later, as a family, we'd watch some TV together, which made my inner-teenager cringe. After that, I'd have a bath and then a final hour of study before bed. The next day, we'd all repeat the whole thing. At twenty-one, I was stuck between being immensely grateful for what I had and shuddering at what life had been reduced to. Oh, the blandness. But put the violins away, for I do not deserve them.

The next morning, on the outward trip with Tom, the subject of mice and men was raised again. This time, the newsreader informed me that a spokesperson from a gay rights group had released a statement: "It seems unlikely that the complexity of human sexuality can be compared to that of a supposedly gay laboratory mouse."

This shit was getting real.

Chapter 2

Serious Simon

Serious Simon is my brother and he's gay. And he's super-serious about being gay. A commercial for breakfast cereal, the symbol on a toilet door, and once, a park swing that was the colour blue—all have been accused of conspiring against him and gay men everywhere. I took my duty, to mercilessly rip the piss out of Simon's seriousness, just as seriously.

"Has there been much progress for the movement of late?" I would enquire, with my most serious and concerned expression. This was a particularly good one, as I coined it on an occasion when he was suffering from constipation, and it also doubled as an enquiry about his almost non-existent sex life.

"Such a shame..." was another good one. Apparently, disapproving people were always condescendingly saying this about Simon and other gay men.

"There's nothing good on TV tonight," and then, after a pause and with a weary tone, "It's such a shame..."

Simon would sigh, and then he'd smile a bit. Once, he fired back: "Not got knocked up in a while, then? No babies going to pop out while I'm here, I hope." A reasonable attempt at a comeback, but I still had a lot to teach him.

The mouse thing was almost too good to be true, and I

had saved it until I next visited his house.

"I don't know if you've heard: They have gay mice now. I don't know exactly how a mouse comes out to the other mice. Apparently, they have organised themselves into a movement. They have a little pink wheel logo and everything."

"It is quite serious actually," he said with a serious expression on his face.

Oh, everything about being gay is, Simon.

"Some scientists up in Edinburgh claim that homosexuality is a disease caused by an imbalance of insulin. They claim that they can test for it–and get this–they can cure it."

In all fairness, that sounded somewhat serious, if true.

Simon's life had gone differently from mine. He did his A-levels, went to University, and then came back a gay man. He mumbled this fact to Mum and Dad, who nodded and said, "Erm, okay." They already knew, because I had told them. Simon had informed me a few months before and I had had a quiet word with them. Being middle class and British is great sometimes. When the big announcement was made, everyone pretended that everyone didn't already know. A few awkward moments, and then, subject changed to football as soon as possible.

I was born in the 1990s, and being homophobic was probably passé for Mum and Dad by the time they had hit University in the 1970s. In all fairness, I think they must have done some hand-wringing about it, behind the scenes. If a son is gay, it's probably going to have some effect on the future family structure, after all. Back then, I couldn't have guessed how much opportunity I was going to get out of the situation for making sport of poor, serious Simon.

Chapter 3

Steven

"There's beggary in love that can be reck-
oned."

Steven, the father of my three-year-old, isn't evil, but he
is completely useless. When I was seventeen, I got caught
up in a romance with him. Walking along the seafront at
midnight he said, "Duya know summat? If I could go out
with anyone in this town, it would be you. I can't see it
happening, mind." Who could resist something like that?

He couldn't see it happening. I was a seventeen-year-
old swot doing her A-levels and he was nineteen (a massive difference at the time) and on the dole and living in
his own flat. At a young age, I felt I had met my other
half. He had the right materials but he needed someone
to fix him up, and he was in luck, because getting things
organised and on-track was my speciality. He struck me
as manly, direct and kind, and I was right about that. If
I'm being honest, the fact that he seemed like a completely
gorgeous, self-assured, masculine man probably blinded
me to his faults.

He was my third boyfriend, but taking him home was
a toughy compared to the others. I don't think anyone in
my family knew anyone who was on the dole. Or covered
in tattoos. Things didn't go as badly as I had feared.

Grandad had been a rigger on the steelworks and Dad appreciated a man's man.

"How the hell are you going to get through life without qualifications or a job?" he berated. "I feel like my daughter's bringing home a layabout." Steven grinned at that, and I could tell that he had never had a bollocking from a dad before, the poor thing. A lot of male behaviour that looks aggressive from the outside is actually affectionate. It's how they play. In fact, the two of them were getting on like a house on fire. My parents recognised a lovely lad who was going through an awkward phase.

However, I could tell what they were thinking: play things wrong, and I'd be pregnant within a couple of months. Very long story short: that's what happened. I still don't understand *how* it happened, because Steven and I were very careful in that regard, and I had always been suspicious of girls who "fell pregnant". Telling my mum was the hardest moment of my life. As it occurred halfway through the year, it seemed that I was ruining my education, the core of the expectations that people had of me. I wavered back forth on the subject, but when I said that I wanted to keep the baby, as we lay together one night, Steven hugged me and said that he wouldn't have it any other way. This commitment and assuredness tipped me in favour of a life-changing decision. I had soon moved into his flat, but what sort of a family would this be?

Steven took drugs. Some days, he'd be fucked up. That meant that he could be found either sitting up while giggling to himself or slumped over, asleep. Other days he'd be fine. In addition, it seems that when you take drugs, you have to sell them and hide them in the flat; that's when you're not stealing them. The most important thing is that you give them away to your mates so that you look like the big man at all times.

To Steven's credit, even before I became pregnant, I don't think I was allowed to take drugs. Maybe it was because he expected immaculate behaviour from his consort, or maybe it was because he loved me?

His friends were awful. He was part of some weird North of England gangster culture in which everyone seemed to think they were a character from a cheesy 80s film. They all fancied themselves as a cross between the stock "cop on the edge" and what gangsters were like in movies. "You got it!", "Ten four, buddy!" and "Let's roll!" were the type of movieland expressions that you'd hear from their stupid mouths. I realised that the men in films were the only positive male role models they had been exposed to. However, that could be said of a lot of young males, and yet not every young man led a lifestyle like Steven's mates. It was a lifestyle fuelled by a welfare situation, one that got better every time they did something wrong.

Their dress style showed off their tattoos and their muscles. I don't understand how they all came to have such big muscles as no one ever went to the gym or owned any weights. I should have made a closer examination of their habits and turned whatever they were doing into a diet plan. It might have been that they did visit the gym and own weights, but admitting to it would have been "gay".

Everyone was a complete fuck-up and no one made any effort to behave sensibly or to better themselves or their situation in any way. All of them were unemployable losers. All of them were idiots. And yet, all of them would run across the road to walk you back to the flat, a friendly arm thrust across your shoulder, as soon as they saw you in the street. All of them were harmless little boys who had lost their way–a happy few, a band of brothers.

For a while, Steven let one of his mates live in the cupboard on the landing outside our flat. For a few quid, his friend was allowed live in the cupboard and sell drugs from it. The dimensions of the cupboard meant that you could sort of sleep in there if you crouched down, and the evidence suggested that he had done just that: he lived and slept in the cupboard. About five local druggies had our door code and would come and go at all hours of the day and night.

"No one will ever know," said Steven. "It's our cupboard."

Hmm... Steven is a business genius whose plans always work, I thought to myself.

One day, when I was about three months pregnant, I was leaving the flat, and the man jumped out of the cupboard.

"Hi?" I said to him.

He was huge, yet emaciated and had little scratches up and down his arms that looked fresh and sticky. He wobbled on his feet and grinned at me, showing me his cracked teeth. There was something unnerving about his teeth that I couldn't put my finger on at first. Afterwards, it occurred to me that they looked like they had been broken by violence and not tooth decay. The man grinned at me as though he were toying with me.

"I'm just off to the shops," I said.

Silence was his reply.

"See ya," I said.

And then he advanced on me, still grinning.

"Erm, actually, I'm just going back in for a minute," I said before bolting back into the flat. I had to stay in the flat for two days, as Steven had disappeared for a while. I phoned my mum and made up the most incredible bullshit to keep her away.

When Steven came back, I told him what happened.

"No problem, babes, I'll have a little word with him." That was good of him. Off he went to have a little word with the drug-dealing, near-catatonic man who lived in our outside cupboard. Half an hour later, he came back. He had broken the skin on his knuckles, as though he had punched something over and over.

"Never see him again, babes." And he was right, I never did.

This was around the time I first caught him being unfaithful to me, and I didn't even catch him, he accidentally confessed to it.

"Where the hell were you? And I want the truth!" I said the next day, locking my eyes on his. I must admit that

I was labouring the point to extract a confession that he had spent two days drinking with his horrible mates. I could hardly believe it when he admitted that he'd been with another woman. Too surprised to be truly angry, I ordered him out of the flat, screaming as I went, arms flailing in his direction. All the time, he was smiling coyly and shaking his head. The situation was amusing to him.

Even when I was throwing him out, I was planning how long I would have to punish him for before I let him back in. This was also the moment I began to realise that we'd both have to pretend that he slept only with me.

When he came back three days later, his mum, June, was with him. As she talked to him, she looked at me imploringly as she explained how sorry he was while slapping him. She wanted to hang on to "Posh Susan", I think. I knew that me and his mum could beat Steven to death with a blunt instrument and he wouldn't raise a finger to defend himself, because it was us.

"Anyway, he knows what he's done, and I'll leave the two of you to talk." Off she went. She'd been through it all too.

Truth time: I did have my share of laughs with the lads. One particular night, we all piled into a MacDonald's around 11pm. Everyone but me was drunk and buzzing on some speed that was going around. The atmosphere was edgy and frightening; not that I was frightened, being within the inner circle.

One of them said to a female member of staff: "I'll have a Big Mac. And I'd like your telephone number please."

She smiled politely and said nothing as the lads stifled their laughter.

After silence from both sides of the counter, she said, still as polite ever: "Can I take your order, sir?"

"Yes... I'd like a big Mac and fries please. Oh, and a coke, if that's okay. Oh... and could I have your telephone number please?"

"I'll take this order," said a male colleague who then took over. He stood there, wrestler-build, arms folded; his annoyance with us was thinly concealed. "Can I take your order, sir?"

"Oh right," said our compatriot, suddenly serious. "Just a Big Mac and fries and a Coke, please mate. Oh... and can I have *your* telephone number? She wouldn't give me hers, and you're a hot piece of ass, if you don't mind me saying so."

So it went on. When it was my turn, I played it straight, but, JD, another one of Steven's mates added, "Could *she* have your telephone number, mate? She's fancied you for ages, but she was too embarrassed to tell ya. Don't ya believe me, mate? Don't ya fancy her?"

Painstakingly, the manager managed to extract our orders from us, and the five of us found somewhere to sit.

There was one other customer, a man with a reflector jacket and cycling gloves.; he looked like he had just come off his shift. He avoided eye contact with our group as they sang rude versions of the song lyrics coming out of the radio. I didn't blame him.

Now and then, one of the guys would walk over to the counter, get the attention of a member of staff and then pretend to forget what he wanted with a slap of his forehead and a "Sorry, mate. It's gone again!" Over and over he did it. There's something about speed that makes repetition seem hilarious and satisfying to the person who's on it.

Before long, one of them came up with a new game: standing on a table and jumping from one to the other. Once he got to the end of the row of tables, he'd run back to his seat, grinning like a naughty schoolboy. Fortunately, the staff were hanging back in the kitchen area by then to avoid the daft remarks and stupid questions that were being flung at them. I didn't blame them either.

Eventually, the guy who was sat on his own put the lid on his plastic cup of tea and walked outside and stood near his bicycle. Obviously, he planned to finish his drink away from us. The lads exchanged looks with each other and

Stephen announced that it was time to go. Before long, they were outside, standing near the man and beaming happily at him. Check and mate. Before long, he put his drink onto one of the tables and cycled off.

The next day, I had sobered up. I hadn't been drunk on alcohol or high on drugs, but I had been under the spell that Stephen's mates had cast. Now, I felt ashamed. The truth was that I had chuckled along with them and made half-hearted signs of disapproval and shock that only worked to egg them on. Would it have been detectable to an outsider that I was not *with them* in any sense? Probably not. Would a show of genuine disapproval on my part have stopped them? Doubtful.

Stephen's friends had played the odds and gamed the system, just like they always did. As obnoxious as they became, there was no chance of them getting into trouble. Even if two policemen had walked into the McDonald's and spotted someone standing on a table and shouting, it wouldn't have been worth bothering with. The chances of them being charged with a crime were practically zero. What had they actually done? They asked a woman for her phone number, stood on a table, sung along with the radio and stood near a man and looked at him. They acted like they were out of control, but they were never out of control; they knew just what they could get away with, and it was always at someone else's expense.

As I sat in bed, that next morning, the spell had broken and I was suffering a hangover of the spirit. I felt sorry for the staff at McDonald's and the man who wasn't allowed to finish his drink.

By the time I was eight months in and ready to pop, I explained to Steven that we were finished.

"Okay, babes, if that's the way it's got to be," he said.

"Babes" he still called me. The whole situation played into his self-image of a drifter outlaw that no woman could ever hold down.

Subsequently, I had to get on with him for the sake of my son. I was determined to go along with the situation because of the experience that I had of living among a community of horrible, yet lovable, fatherless men like Steven.

As far as I can see, the effects of fatherlessness can vary. Steven's brother John is pretty much the opposite of Steven. John works as a lab technician. So, he has a job, for a start. John always has a joke up his sleeve. However, he's older than Steven and he experienced a period of a fairly stable family life, and I think that made a difference.

I wish that I was attracted to a good-hearted, fat, funny bloke like John. I don't think that John has it made, though. I think that there is a seriousness underneath the act that only I can detect. He must be lonely. Steven burst into laughter when I asked him if John had ever had a girlfriend: "I don't know and I don't ask."

No lecturing from Mum and Dad when I had to return home, bless them. I moved back into my old bedroom, and we made Simon's old room into a nursery.

There was no point in trying to get anything out of Steven, money-wise. Mum and Dad had to do the financial heavy-lifting while I was living at home with baby. My friends were all delighted to leave Cleethorpes, a seaside town on the east coast where I have lived my entire life. I am sure that the pace of life is more exciting in one of the cities, and I would like to experience it for myself one day. But as places to be stuck go, Cleethorpes is not bad at all.

Simon started paying some money into my bank account as soon as I split with Steven. Sometimes I'd sigh because it seemed too much. It's never been discussed, and Simon could rip me to shreds if he ever wanted to by rubbing my nose in it, but he never would. Between Simon, Mum and Dad and welfare benefits, I have it pretty good. The money enables me to do my Open University course, look after baby and (just) run a car. I made some dodgy life decisions, but everything was manageable because of my family. Everything was fine

Steven

before the mice turned gay.

Chapter 4

It's a thing

The mouse business was soon officially a thing on the Internet. #gaycure became a hashtag on Twitter. Other people had picked up on the mouse. After pranksters turned the Deadmou5 logo pink and rechristened it Gaymou5, it started popping up all over the place. The story coasted along as a talking point and a bit of joke for a few weeks, but then the BBC reported on it as part of the main evening news, and later, announced a forthcoming documentary about it.

The story was that some scientists in Edinburgh had carried out some experiments on mice. When the scientists gave a large dose of insulin to the mice in their food, a number of the mice began to engage in same-sex sexual activity. Out of ten male mice, eight of them showed an interest in copulating with other males, atypical behaviour in mice. The behaviour ceased when the insulin dosage was lowered.

Shortly afterwards, the National Health Service began trials of a new oral insulin delivery method in a hospital in Manchester. Sure enough, when questioned, the men and women reported an increase in sexual interest towards members of the same sex. In fact, one of them had gone to the press to complain about the effect on his marriage.

A week after that, there were two new developments,

and the first of these had just the right amount of juice for the tabloids: A secondary school headmaster, who had been on the oral insulin delivery trial, had left his wife for a man. Grainy, long-range photographs clearly showed him getting into a car with another man, confirming the story. That article also featured a photograph of the semi-detached house that he had lived in with his wife. The house gave no outward signs of anything unusual.

The second development was that another man who had been on the trial had committed suicide.

As per our tradition, Simon picked me up on Thursday night. Then, back to his house for Gay Club. I'm not allowed to call it that, as it's Simon's "sexuality encounter group". Four or five of his gay friends talking about being gay while I try to not be too sarcastic. My life was very exciting. What can I tell you? There was pizza.

Gay rights activists are generally on the side of right and do some good, but they aren't, collectively speaking, famed for their humour. Simon's friends, like Simon himself, had homosexuality as both their sexual orientation and their hobby. He'd been through a few different organisations since Uni, but I suspect that they weren't serious enough for him, so he started organising his own meetings at his place. I did sometimes wonder if some of these guys could, y'know, try being gay together, as in having sexual relationships with each other. However, I knew I'd get shot for suggesting it; gay sex was frowned upon as a subject of debate at Gay Club.

At least there was one other person with a sense of humour there. Is it being condescending towards a gay person to think, *What a shame...* about someone, because you'd be in like a shot if they weren't gay? That's what I thought when I first met Gary. In many ways, Gary is the opposite of Steven. He's unmanly, without being effeminate. He has lovely long blond hair down to his waist and he is whip-thin. I loved beating him at arm wrestling, and he took his defeats with good grace.

Once, I enquired, "You're *sure* that is your wanking arm, Gary?"

"You're just not doing it enough. You need to ask him for some tips," I continued, pointing at Simon.

Serious Simon had to bring his brat sister into his club house, and then she started mentioning wanking. Awesome burgers. Sighs all round, smiles from me. That sort of thing never got old. For me. In addition, I enjoyed turning the subject to wanking, something I knew a great deal about.

Once, I had to get the bus back home and Gary walked with me to the station. As part of a joke, I put my arm around Gary, and then something brilliant happened: A gang of young lads were hanging around the station, and one of them shouted, "Lesbos!" at us. Major embarrassment when Gary turned around to look at them. The expression on the young lad's face was priceless. I think that, for some men, being mistaken for a woman would have been the ultimate insult. Such men would have felt compelled to go over and pummel the person who shouted the comment.

"We're not lesbos, because he's a man," I said, to stick up for Gary. If I'd really wanted to punish the cocky little sod, I would have approached him and explained what the actual situation was until his brain went pop considering it.

Gary thought it was great, whisper-shouting "Oi, Lesbos!" all the way to the bus terminal, and the incident was often recounted for humorous effect.

So, in summary, I didn't have a full-blown crush on Gary, because I knew there is no point.

Oh Gary, be my mate, please, I'd sometimes think. I dearly wished that Simon would have a go, but advice or commentary from me on Simon's no-sex life was a no go area.

My arrival at Gay Club would typically be accompanied by sighs, but that was usually played for humour. Even Gary would join in, grimacing and saying, "To make matters worse..." upon seeing me. This time, for the first time, I genuinely felt unwelcome. Later, I would realise that it was because the ground had begun to shift under their feet.

Gary was speaking: "So, all my memories–a lifetime of memories–of being gay would be wiped? It's ridiculous. Or, would my memories suddenly become abhorrent to me? I don't suppose a straight man would like to remember all the times he went to bed with another man."

One of you lot has been to bed with a man? I didn't dare interject. I sensed that it wouldn't be appreciated.

"Perhaps I could take some pills to change my taste in music?" added Rob, a young Jimmy Somerville look-a-like who made Simon seem like a non-serious gay person.

When Rob said this, I began to wonder if it *would* be possible to take a pill that would change a person's taste in music. A brain works on chemicals, connections between cells and electrical impulses; it's a machine, it's not magical. While the others debated, I worked on this idea further. If I were in a subdued mood, I might be less inclined to hear energetic music. Could a pill make me feel subdued? Yes. I was oversimplifying like mad, but in that contrived example, a pill had altered my taste in music.

There was a break in the conversation, so I ventured: "Isn't it too early to be taking this so seriously? Frankly, it sounds like a crank theory."

"That's easy for you to say, since it doesn't concern you," Gary snapped. My lovely Gary. He was shaken up. They all were. These events had a familiar signature for many of them. A little bell rang to remind them, on some level, of past battles, those of sexual realisation and of coming out.

For the rest of the night, the four of them pushed the implications back and forth between them; it continued to amaze me that it had caught their imagination to such an extent. Sarcastic Susan knew when her brand of piss-taking wasn't in demand, so I hung around in the kitchen.

The conclusion, after over two hours of discussion? The discovery was nonsense and the product of quackery, but that it was also an attack on gay people, as it had so readily caught the public imagination. At all times, I was aware that the announcement had injected something into the air and had a surprising effect on the group. Gary had snapped at me, but I could see that everyone was under pressure.

Simon was silent, obviously deep in thought, as we drove back to Mum and Dad's. I knew that this would be one of a few crank medical discoveries announced in the press that year. To the media, the scientific validity of this theory was less important than its entertainment value, and yes, the humour of it did demean homosexuality and play on latent homophobia. And yet, for some reason, the idea had music to it. Why was it catching on in the way it had?

Chapter 5

A room of one's own

I am ashamed to say that a year after the baby was born, I had no close friends apart from my brother. My pregnancy had occurred at just the wrong moment and I had to leave sixth form to have the kid. Crucially, this meant that I lost connection with all of my friends. I heard less and less from them over the course of the next year, and the year after that, they had all moved on to University.

There was a stigma surrounding the stupid girl who had got pregnant, part of which was daft and part of which I understood. The daft part was that everyone automatically assumes that a woman must have been irresponsible to have become unexpectedly pregnant. I took every reasonable precaution and I wasn't doing anything that most of my classmates weren't doing when they were seventeen.

The part I do understand is that some of the other girls would have been in the same position as me and made the opposite decision so that they could continue with the normal course of their lives. Odd Girl did something that must have seemed strange, and even I will never know if it was the right decision; that's a hard thing for a mother to admit. All of my friends came from a similar background and they had much the same future planned out. That I did had forced them to confront something about themselves. I insulted their values of modernity and of "getting on". Looking back, I don't know what my plan was, but I know that I must have had a crap taste in friends. I bet none of them could have put into words what I had done wrong if someone asked them.

During the final few visits, my friends were embarrassed. By then, they were all off, living in the University halls and I was living, largely, in my bedroom. What a huge gulf between lifestyles. When the last of them made a final visit, we sat in my bedroom, baby asleep. At that point, who were we, the two of us? She had been a girl that I took to McDonald's as a treat on my birthday. By the time of that last visit, were we girls, or were we sophisticated young women? In some respects, I was the adult now, more than her, because I was someone's mother. It was confusing. And embarrassing. Being middle class, educated and living at home in your twenties gifts you with a magical field of embarrassment that is active at all times. A visit to me must have been like visiting a relative in prison. I have no doubt that they all kept back much of the exciting news of their adventures, as it must have seemed cruel to mention everything they got up to.

I had a few acquaintances from Gay Club and from elsewhere, but no one that I would call a close friend. How shameful. Why is it that I wouldn't feel the same sense of shame about my position if I were to announce that I was randy, desperate for a shag, and on the pull? I was desperate for the simple, satisfying friendships of my youth. I sometimes think that I am not that likeable. Neither men nor women appreciate sarcasm as much as they should.

And yet, guilt slapped me in the face. I had everything so good, and so little of it had been due to my own efforts. I felt guilty about having something as lovely as my room. As well as being my bedroom, it also served as my study, and when I was inside it, studying, I was in my element. I had my own kettle up there and I brought up everything I needed to keep me supplied with coffee (decaf) as I worked on my coursework. I was, in part, motivated by a mixture of guilt alongside gratitude towards my family, but the truth is that I loved working on my degree.

There's a thought: perhaps my subjects, anthropology and sociology, had made me one of the enemy, representative of the scientists who had been churning things up at Gay Club. I quickly dismissed the next thought I had, to study the effect of the discovery on a community of homosexual men. Studying your own life or the people close to you is generally considered a no-no. There would be no shutting down of that part of my brain, though.

Already, I was too much of an observer of life rather than a participant in it. Like Simon. He wanted to examine and debate things rather than go out and do them. I wasn't engaging much, socially, but I had an excuse. What was his? He has a good job, his own place and is gay. Cleethorpes, where we all live, isn't exactly a world-renowned gay Mecca, but it's not too bad.

When I was ten and Simon was fourteen, a computer entered our lives. Before that, Dad had an old one in the study, but the new computer we got as a family one Christmas lived in the dining room so that everyone could use it. The big difference was that this one came with an AOL account, and therefore, the Internet. Simon and I got on fairly well until then, but limited computer time soon developed into a huge source of friction. If my mum had been a character in a sitcom, her catchphrase would have been, "I wish we'd never got that thing!"

I loved playing games like DooM and looking things up on the web. For Simon, it quickly became his entire world. At the weekend, he could easily sit on it for twelve hours at a time. That doesn't seem amazing these days, but back then there was no Facebook, YouTube or Twitter.

Despite being a teacher, Mum still has a lot of the working class accent. I regularly take her off by saying, "I don't want you looking at girls on that thing!" followed up with "Yes, mum!" in a squeaky voice. It has lightened many a quiet moment between Simon and I. Was he looking at guys on the Internet when he had a private moment on the computer? I know I bloody was.

In an attempt to ease the squabbling and to navigate this sudden shift in teenage lifestyles, my mum declared that we could use it on alternate hours.

"What? I often need more than a single hour at time," said Simon. "Very well. I'll have the even hours. It will give me the hour before school."

"No!" said Mum. "No more using it before school. Me and your Dad need to be able to hear from work." Back then, Internet access meant blocking up the phone.

Simon kept his even hours designation and then started getting up at 6am or earlier to get in some extra time. I loved using a computer, but Simon liked the computer itself, sometimes taking it to bits to fiddle with it. It may have been his way of retreating from the heterosexual world imposed on a fourteen-year-old school boy. By the time he started sixth form college, it was obvious that his life was going to revolve around computers. Simon had "found himself", sitting in a computer science class, holding court with the mates he now had.

Chapter 6

The dark mouse rises

I had just been slapped in the face. Not literally, of course. Apparently, at Gay Club, I was now the enemy.

When you know that you're going into battle, you can set your face in a neutral expression in advance, but this was an unexpected attack from an unexpected direction. That evening, the talk at Bender Central was still all about the "gay cure"; even they had begun to use the tabloid term. Everyone was taking themselves and the situation much too seriously. So, to lighten the mood, I put my arm around Gary's shoulder.

"Surely, anything that can reduce the gay scourge is a positive development," says I, for a joke. Oops. Not the right thing to say.

Firstly, I discovered, I am a "slut". Secondly, it must be easy being me because I just have to get pregnant if I need more money. What the hell? I may have actually flinched when Gary said it. Delay between looking hurt and looking incredulous: about two full seconds, way too long to pull it off convincingly. I had overstepped the mark with my joke at completely the wrong time. But when I put my arm around someone, I don't expect to be attacked. From there on, the match was lost.

Rob had been waiting for this moment for about three years, and he now had his chance. "I don't even know why she comes here," he said with a solemn tone of resignation. Bastard.

I'd regained some composure and my eyes flicked to Simon who began to speak: "Fuck off, Rob. And that's a bit strong, Gary. Everyone needs to calm down."

Not bad, I thought to myself. *Not great, but a reasonable start.*

And then my beloved brother turned to me and said, "In all fairness, your comments *are* wearing a bit thin. This might be a joke for you... "

I couldn't believe what I was hearing. All I could do was say, "Oh, all right then." My voice didn't wobble too much. To save face, I stayed for another five minutes and then made an excuse to catch the bus back.

On the way home, I fantasised about telling them to fuck off when they made their apologies. I was going to enjoy this, so I made sure the ringer on my phone was turned up, not wanting miss the call on the noisy bus. By the time I was home, I decided I might have to curtail their punishment period. They were obviously operating under extraordinary stress due to unusual circumstances. I'd try to take that into account when they rang me.

"Not going to Simon's this week, love?" asked mum, when she saw me in the kitchen the following Thursday.

"I'm a bit bogged under with coursework this week, actually," I lied.

To be fair to them, the pressure had been turned up by mouse–that's what everyone called the drug cocktail that turns you straight. None of the ingredients were technically illegal and loads of people were making themselves sick eating things that contained glucose. Diabetics and people suffering from hypoglycaemia had been warned not to take their medication out in public and to store it in a secure place.

Mouse talk was everywhere, and I'd experienced the effect of these new developments, on gay people, first hand. The biggest surprise was that this discovery had uncovered a demand for sexuality reorientation, and that was interpreted as a massive insult to gay people. The term taken up by almost the entire media, the "gay cure", summed up the whole problem: some people still thought that being gay was wrong, and therefore something to be cured.

There had been a noticeable shift in attitudes. A Daily Mail journalist opined: "My sympathy with homosexuals would be diminished if being gay turned out to be optional." Admittedly, this was no wet liberal, but even so, it was a surprisingly stark opinion on homosexuality to see in a newspaper article. This was someone who had been forced to keep his disapproval to himself in the past; he wouldn't have dared say it in print until a few weeks ago. This hinted at the real problem: for people of my generation, homophobia may have seemed unjust, but more than anything, it seemed uncool. The recent groundswell of anti-homosexual feeling in newspaper articles revealed what some people had really been thinking all along.

Political correctness had a lot to answer for if this was the end result of not being able to say anything bad about being gay for thirty years. Preventing discourse had not changed attitudes, it would seem, not deep down. The comments beneath online articles, the modern equivalent of pub-talk, were mostly awful. Something had been unleashed. Obviously, the websites of some papers were worse than others, but they were all at it.

"Finally, some common sense on this issue!" from a man who'd been waiting fourty years to say his piece, he claimed, although he wasn't specific about what his point actually was. In more normal times, I would have repeated that in front of Seriously Gay for comic effect.

Seeing "It's about time. We'll soon be rid of them forever," modded up to the high heavens made me cringe. People suggesting that they will be able to get men tested for it before they can work with children, ditto.

"They should put this in the water supply of schools rather than encouraging it like they do now," sounded as crazy and baffling as, "At least the taxpayer won't have to pay for them any more." Huh?

One man said in his comment, "I am a gay man and

I would be interested in this, if it works." Fair enough, I suppose.

Something else had been bothering me, and it too related to political correctness. My mum was as PC as you could get. I remember her warning the young Simon that he shouldn't be looking at porn on the Internet. He had looked embarrassed and she had smiled.

That she enjoyed the situation had not registered with me until that moment, five years later.

If he had come out while he was still a schoolboy, I think his home life would have been much better than he might have imagined, due to Mum and Dad. But would Mum have issued a similar warning telling him that he mustn't look at naked men on the Internet? It seemed like a double standard. In fact, if she had caught me having a look, would she have given me the same smirking lecture?

Porn is, if we're being honest, consensual sex. If Mum would have been unwilling to criticise her daughter or a gay man for looking at it, she should have shown her seemingly straight son the same respect for his sexuality. Were moments like that, ironically, part of what made him keep his sexuality a secret?

Conclusions: a huge number of people still considered being a gay a fault; they were willing to say it when they thought they could without chastisement; a casual lack of respect for other people's sexual goings on had always existed.

Understandably, gay people felt embattled, but they were not, as a group, free from fault in this matter, either. All of the discussions had revealed a stubbornness on their part. The party line had been, at least with Simon's crowd, that you were born gay. So, therefore the determiner was biological rather than social. According to them, nothing could change it or prevent it.

Okay, let's look at that. If it is something within the biology of your body (chemicals, hormones, genetics, or neurons within your brain) why is it impossible to change it? It seemed to me that it would be easier to change something that was physical rather than something that was psychological. I mean, how do you unbake a cake?

Perhaps a person's sexuality is something that develops as a result of formative experiences or adherence to social norms? So, a social and psychological rather than a biological determiner. As a heterosexual, I don't have a problem with that. Perhaps my sexuality would have been different if I had been exposed to a different set of experiences.

I had boyfriends before Steven, and I had sex with them, but Steven was my first real love. In all fairness to him, he is lovable despite his faults, but I'm not sure that he is who I would choose to fall in love with. Steven's sheer masculinity was part of the attraction, I am sure. But did Disney cartoons and Star Wars impose an ideal upon me at an early age? There was no doubt that Steven was, utterly, a rogue. I don't find such a theory, when applied to my sexual orientation, either offensive or unlikely. Neither would I be offended if it became settled science that my sexual preferences were shaped by genetics.

Over and over again, truisms as well as lies were stirring things up, and more was yet to come.

"Fuck off," I texted to Gary. As in, *please be nice and be my giggling partner again.* Nothing.

Chapter 7

The age of reverse-mouse

I'm happy to see Simon when he comes for a visit at Mum and Dad's, but part of me doesn't like it. Again, the sensation was of having skipped a groove in life. Twenty-one years old, a mother, and I still felt like a little kid, hanging around in the lounge while Mum cooked the dinner. I might have wondered whether I would have been better off in a flat on the dole and living the life of a young adult, but I felt a noble sense of penance from my lot; I'd mucked things up in life, and now I was going to do what it took to get my head back above water.

Up in my room with the door shut, I didn't have the guts to mention Gay Club. The secret truth was that I had almost no social life, and losing the encounter group had been a blow. What a shame that it had come to this, being dependent on Gay Club and having let everything else fall apart. When you're a child, you are shoved around from one place to another and that becomes your social scene. Making a few friends at school or at Girl Guides seems very involved, but it is relatively effortless. I had no doubt that this continued to be the case for my erstwhile peers who were living large at Uni.

I had built up the same instincts and life strategies as

anyone else, but they weren't very effective now. Drifting along and waiting for chemistry to take its course as part of a social scene is considerably more difficult as an adult. Here I was, a Nowhere Girl, twenty-one years old and with no peer group at all. Even if I could patch things up with the guys, what I had with them was insufficient for a woman in her twenties. I was going to have to do something, to make an effort on my own behalf. Somehow.

It transpired that things were weren't irreparably damaged, anyway.

Simon laughed. "You'll probably want to stay away this week. Everyone is up in arms about mouse."

That was it? I had thought I was ex-communicated for life. A few words and a laugh and everything was alright again. Oh, of course: Simon would fix it, and everyone would have to start putting up with the brat sister again. I had, perhaps, built the whole thing up in my mind too much, but once again, I had escaped disaster thanks to a family that loved me. Cringe.

"Whatever," I replied, ultra-cool.

"Things have gone up a notch anyway. Have you heard of reverse-mousing?"

"No."

"They now reckon that you can go the other way—from straight to gay."

That was interesting. Until now, everyone had forgotten that the original experiment had, supposedly, made the mice gay. Why did all thoughts leap to making gay people straight rather than the other way round? In humans, also, the initial reports were of people being turned gay. One difference was that, historically, there *have* been systematic efforts to enforce heterosexuality onto people. Straight equals "normal", in a lot of situations in society, and for that reason, no one considered the possibility of people wanting to be gay.

"I'm glad I'm not able attend at the moment," I said. "My take on this is a bit different from theirs."

"How so?"

"Firstly, I'm not buying this for a moment. I don't think

the science is there. Yet, they've all accepted it as real. I find that odd in itself. It's as though they've all been caught out in a guilty secret or something, hence the anger. Secondly–and I don't think this would make me popular with your little mates–I don't have a problem with the discovery, if it is true."

"Well, it's a bit different for you."

"What's that got to do with anything? Pointing out that I'm an outsider is just another way of saying: 'You're objective about things.' I would agree that mouse has churned things up and revealed some nasty attitudes that had been masked by political correctness until now. I agree that's an unfortunate aspect."

Simon tutted at that. "An unfortunate aspect."

"There you go again. I'm being objective about it, and I don't think that makes me wrong. The gay militants that you hang around with–pseudo-militant in their sad little discussion group–have always insisted that you're born gay or straight or bisexual. Therefore, sexual orientation must have a physical basis rather than a social one. This means that it must be genetic, and therefore, expressed through the way someone's brain is wired up, or the chemicals floating around inside their body."

"Who says it does work like that?"

"Well, loads of gay activists, for a start. It could even be a combination of factors. But even if that is the case, surely it could then be altered by altering the factors that *determine* sexual orientation?" I let that idea sit for a moment. "However–and I think that this is part of what has got everyone so wound up–they've never had to be specific before. The majority of the most vocal activists have always said that you're born straight or gay and that nothing can change that fact. Okay, but what is the basis for that determiner? They've never had to explain how it worked."

I'd been considering this a lot, and now, I had the floor. Standing in my bedroom. Underneath a Radiohead poster.

Now in full flight, I continued, "And this brings us to

the unmentionable alternative: That it isn't physically determined from birth. Perhaps it is psychologically determined and affected by social factors."

This made Simon wince a little. He shook his head.

"You don't like that? Well, Simon, that doesn't make any difference. It could well be true."

We both knew that this was a very difficult area for the gay community. If true, the social environment could shape a person's sexual orientation. It was a major taboo, particularly for gay men. Both explanations opened up the floodgates, leading to the worst thing that a gay person could hear: that there was something *wrong* with being gay, that it was something to be cured or prevented. From an early age, boys are told to "be a man" about things. "Boy's don't cry," they are told. And do you know why? Because if they did cry, they might end up growing up to be a poof.

I never understood the idea of homosexuality as being effeminate. I'd met quite a few gay people, because of Simon, and a lot of them seemed very masculine. For one thing, the act of getting into bed with another man seemed, to me, very manly in itself.

Every gay man seemed to have a recognisable strategy and a place within the hierarchy. Stereotypes crop up for a reason. I wondered where I fitted into all of this. Did I play a part that an outsider would be able to identify? Young Woman Who Gets Away With Murder? *Stop it, brain.* Would I ever escape from my attraction to Hyper Masculine Rogue? *I said, stop it!*

Simon didn't fit into any of the standard personae, and I think that this limited his ability to get on with (or get off with) other gay people, apart from his sad, sexless circle of similar blokes. He was a lovely looking young man, but Nice Young Man didn't seem to chime with gay people. As far as I knew, he had *done it*, in terms of a couple of shags here and there. But why did I think that he would have been on about his fourth long-term relationship by now if he was straight? He was a bit boring, but a lovely person, and basically, a great catch for some lucky female.

It wasn't for Nowhere Girl, stuck at home with a kid, to tell Simon how life should be lived, but I wanted to hear tales of him piling out of the pub with his mates. Hear about it? I wanted to be with him, laughing away, egging him on to ask out the latest guy of his dreams. If only I could enforce a "no more Gay Club" rule on all of us. Gay Club was a nice, comfortable situation that was holding us back. And what did they really get out of it? I bet a discussion like the one Simon and I were having would have been verboten at their discussion group.

"How would you feel if this were about you?" asked Simon, breaking the thoughtful silence.

"I'd be fine with it," I replied, already having the answer up my sleeve. "Perhaps my sexual orientation comes from biology. Or, perhaps it's psychological. I don't care. I do suspect it's a *combination* of biology and psychology." I was on fire and on point. Then my mum shouted and called us for tea, which made me whither somewhat. Simon didn't even smirk. Good old Simon.

Later that week, a horrible woman in *The Guardian* reported that she had put herself on the mouse. Reverse-mouse, in her case. I say that she's horrible because she's got it in for men, a species that I have some affection for. As ever, she felt that all of her problems had been caused by men. As ever, it seemed to me that all of her problems were self-created or entirely in her own head.

The article was called "Mouse Works–I Am On it!". "I've had it with men," her essay began. Fairly standard for her. She felt that reverse-mouse had given her a glorious stepping off point from which she could say goodbye to men forever.

If it works, it will be a glorious day of celebration for the men, I thought.

Her and another woman were taking insulin together as part of her plan. Her story, and her experiment, I had to admit, were intriguing.

She described sitting across from her friend after they had both taken the stuff, which they had baked into cookies. I was surprised that she was willing to oppress herself into undertaking something as domestic as baking a cookie, but great change requires great sacrifices.

She noticed the first effects after about half an hour. Initially, she became aware of a change in her partner's appearance.

> Her skin looked soft and beautifully lumines-cent. Before, I had secretly shared society's view that my old friend was overweight, but now, her body looked full and intriguing. What a wonderful world–that of the woman's body–that we could now explore together. I reached out with a hand and stroked her face. What a soft and lovely thing it was. I asked her how it felt, but for her, the effect was not as pronounced. This, I concluded, may have been because it was our first time reverse-mousing.

> I reached over and kissed her and felt some-thing I had never managed to feel with a man. She backed away. It was obviously too soon for her to explore this side of her feelings. "What does my body feel like?" I asked her. She reached across and grabbed my breast. Oh, what a feeling! Intriguingly, she reported that, to her, it felt very much like one of her own and "sort of rubbery". The physical part was obviously taking longer for her accept. We may have to up the dose for our next experiment.

Hmm... I thought to myself. *Could it be that you are a conflicted lesbian, Julie, and your friend isn't one? It would certainly explain a lot of your problems, including– according to your constant reports on the matter–getting little or no enjoyment out of sex with all of the "useless men" that you have been with.*

Even if this did work, what was their long-term plan for each other? Would they have to have cookies each

morning and be lesbians all day, or would they save it for
the weekend?

Clearly, she felt a huge relief, now that she had the
solution to all of her problems. She said that she had
already begun to look at the local property market so that
they could get a place together.

The rest of the article explained her grander plan. Now
that the basic problem of sexual partnership had been
solved for people like her, there would be no need for
men at all. Reproduction would be handled by storing
up sperm and keeping a few men around to maintain the
supplies. She ended by outlining a wondrous future in
which women would take command of humankind.

What annoyed me most about Julie was that if she had
it in for any other group of people, such as gay people or
Jews, someone like her would be calling for her head.

Chapter 8

Gary

Simon rang me at 7:30am and told me to get Mum to take the kids to school. He would pick me up as soon as possible and take me to the hospital.

"Gary isn't very well," he said.

I tried to say "Right?" without saying, *What does that have to do with me?*

"Look, it concerns you. I'll explain when I get there."

Oh crap. Oh crap. Oh crap.

I told mum that one of Simon's friends was in the hospital and that I was needed for some reason. Mum was curious for details, but I batted her off and headed for the shower. Quick shower, quick breakfast, anything to fill up the time a bit. Sitting in the lounge was hellish, so I waited outside on the path.

It was obviously a suicide attempt, and me texting "Fuck off" must be have been a factor. That was the only possible explanation. What puzzled me was why they needed me at the hospital. Did they want me to apologise to him?

Simon turned up and we drove off in silence. His expression seemed neutral. That must have meant that he didn't know about the text.

"So, what's this about?" I ventured. I hadn't expected him to smile when he looked at me, but he did. Then he explained what was going on. What a weird, weird situation even for the post-mouse age that we were living in.

"Oh right, so I've got to go all the way back on my own?" I mock-protested at Simon as he dropped me off at the bus terminal two hours later. By then, I was off the hook, and Sarcasm Girl had regained her powers. It wasn't suicide and it was weird, but it wasn't, technically, my fault. Oh, and Gary was all right as far as I could see. The sudden feeling of elation was mixed in with other emotions that would take a while to process.

By the time we arrived at the hospital, Simon had filled me in on what had happened to Gary. It seemed that he had taken some glucose medication that he nicked from a relative to become straight. To be with me. That's right, I was his ideal partner. It might have been the deepest flattery I had ever received.

When Simon and I arrived at Gary's bedside, he looked embarrassed. I'm not surprised, this was someone finding out you fancy them, times ten.

"He's been very stupid indeed," the doctor told us in a weary voice. "He's lucky he didn't kill himself. He did have enough sense to call someone before he passed out."

Simon added, "It's lucky that he managed to get the door open before he fell unconscious. He was lying half way out. I thought he'd tried to kill himself!"

"I did ring to tell you what had happened," said Gary.

"I do remember hearing something about a mouse," was Simon's reply to that. "But you're lucky I even bothered going to see you. I nearly didn't. I thought you were drunk." Overall, we kept things light, as we were both relieved that he was alright.

The doctor changed her tone to one that made us all feel like we were about twelve. "He's probably going to be okay. There should be no lasting effects, but–and I want you all to hear this–he mustn't ever try something like this again."

It was difficult to tell what her take on it was. It could have been either: *daft kids messing around with drugs* or *idiots not accepting their sexuality in this day and age.*

"I won't," said Gary with a groggy resignation, and we all believed that it would be his last experiment with mousing it.

We engaged in half an hour or so of mostly cautious talk. However, I did take my turn to lecture by pointing out that part of the problem was that they spent all this time talking about being gay in a way that never got personal.

"Simon, you've got such a stick up your arse about the politics of being gay. Neither of you talk about yourselves. And in a way, I think that's how you both like things. But Gary isn't some shut-in that doesn't know anyone else who's gay. He goes to a discussion group, every week, year after year, and look how he's ended up."

Even Simon reluctantly nodded along with that. Before we left, I gave Gary a kiss on the forehead. It felt like kissing a friend rather than kissing a sexy man.

Once on the bus, with time alone to think, I considered Gary's turmoil and that I was at the centre of it. Susan Embarrassingly No Mates had someone else who though she was pretty great after all. There was just one problem: she was a woman and he was a gay man.

Being analytical, I considered that there have to be four points of attraction in every romantic relationship. Partner A must be *romantically* attracted to partner B, and the same must be true, vice versa. That makes two points of attraction that have to be fulfilled. In addition, there has to be *sexual* attraction between partners A and B. So, that is another two points of attraction that have to be met.

What was going on here? Given the right encouragement, no problem with the sexual attraction between Gary and I, from my side, and that's one of the essential points satisfied. From there on it starts to get (more) complicated. I liked Gary and I'm sure that, if he was a heterosexual man who liked me, the romantic side would be there too. But this means that there is a third force in play, besides the romantic and sexual forms of attraction. This force must be friendship, in many ways the least understood and most underrated, culturally. Gary and I seemed to have potential for that in buckets. So, that adds up to six potential points of attraction that I could think of straight away.

Other uneven relationships existed. For example, if a man went with a prostitute; sex was had, and the whole arrangement constituted a relationship of sorts. In that example, simple sexual attraction of the man for the woman, along with a desire for money on her part, was enough to keep things going.

However, if you examine the example of a marriage that doesn't run on sex, things are a bit different. A woman might marry someone, that she likes, but that she doesn't find that attractive. But there would, typically, be at least *some* sexual compatibility between the two of them. I'm sure that there are many marriages that are long-lasting and "successful" in which there is friendship, but no romance, along with only limited compatibility on the sexual front.

There *are* relationships that survive because of sex and nothing else. In the example of the prostitute and her client, sex plus money were two sides of the equation that balance each other out. Every relationship type that is commonplace must be the result of a workable equilibrium.

It seemed that Gary liked me enough to risk his safety and turn his world upside down to have a relationship with me. What a compliment. As it stood, unless mouse worked, which I was finding increasingly unlikely, we had the beginnings of the mysterious, little-understood *friendship* component. Whatever happened, I was going to pursue that one now. We'd both been too shy to in the past. I wanted, I had told him, for him to come to my house and go places with me.

I got the impression that, fifty years ago, we might have had a lot of what it took to make even marriage work. However, there was a problem in the case of a male.

I wouldn't be interested in, for example, marriage to a man who couldn't achieve arousal, as the sex would be impossible or incomplete. Asking him to lie back and to think of England wouldn't work for us. Or, not for me.

I looked at the relationship I was forced to now maintain with Steven. Probably, I would not choose him as a friend; the magic just wasn't there. But I had been attracted to him, and I do feel that if a few things had been different, the relationship, as a couple, could have sustained itself and even blossomed.

Gary could have been successful in his gay to straight conversion, only to find that he didn't fancy me, as a straight man.

Gary and I were more similar than I had realised until that day. I don't like "girly" things and he doesn't particularly like being a bloke. No wonder he could never find anyone, he didn't have much in common with the tiny pool of possibilities from Gay Club. No wonder I found it difficult to find friends, I preferred hanging out with a bunch of guys. That was my epiphany. I was a friendbian, I prefer male friends.

How much each of these factors play into each other is hard to say. I had wished, before it seemed like a real possibility, that Gary was straight. Maybe mouse could work or would be perfected one day, and he could make a proper attempt at sexuality reassignment, if he still wanted to. But what if we just didn't have what it takes once he had done it?

Part II

John's homosexual gamble

Chapter 9

Don't doubt the mouse

I was a thirty-year-old man, working as a lab equipment technician, and I hated my life. Saying that to myself made me feel a bit better about things.

I'm going to tell you what happened on the day I found out about the mice. I couldn't help but feel excited as I drove home that evening. I have heard that people who are planning to commit suicide can feel a sense of elation about it, and that's how I felt. Things weren't going that well, in general, and I didn't even know if what I had in mind was going to work, but at least I had a plan.

I've never felt suicidal; perhaps it's something genetic. I always seemed to get pushed down until I was on the floor, and that's where I spent most of my life. People who knew me would have been surprised to learn that I lived on the floor because I was good at fooling them. I always had a joke up my sleeve, and that makes me the fat, funny lab tech; as I went from chemist to chemist, they expected it from me.

"This should be completely safe for you now... Oh no, something's gone wrong!" I exclaimed before grabbing onto the desk and falling over. The back room staff at the chemist were laughing at the beginning, but seeing the funny fat equipment tech fall over and begin writhing about, while clutching his throat, pushed them over the edge.

"This guy's crazy!" one of them said to her pal.

Hey, as women are always going on about how much they like a sense of humour in a man, why doesn't one of you ask me out? I didn't reply to them both. There was no point, as I was the epitome of everything women say they like and actually don't like.

At my next stop, I flipped my magnifying visor down.

"I'm going to take you both home with me and perform experiments on you. Come along now," I said in a creepily serious voice. More laughs. More insulin. I've been stealing it for a while, ever since I found out about reverse-mousing. They keep a careful tally of all drugs in a place like that, but once I'm backstage, as it were, I can take anything I like, if I'm careful.

I was sick of women. I didn't hate them or anything, but I was sick of being completely sexually inert around them. I didn't feel like I deserved to be a huge success, but I thought that I deserved something.

A few months before mouse emerged, I had taken a trip down the pub with the lads from work. It was late opening and a couple of women were shouting over the music in the beer garden. They were drunk, they were crass, and yet, they were both pretty. Single mothers blowing off steam would have been my guess. I had very little banter in a situation like that. It was the type of environment that stifled my main asset, my humour.

Nigel, one of the other techs was chatting to one of them. "Nothing embarrasses you, does it, love?"

"Well, I don't know—is this embarrassing?" she said with a puzzled expression on her face. And then she lifted up her top to give us all a look, to the accompaniment of cheers from the lads.

For me, it was an ambition finally realised. I was thirty years old and that was my first look at a pair of breasts. As I had expected, seeing breasts in real life was different from seeing them on a screen or in print.

The next couple of weeks were an emotional roller coaster for me. I knew this would happen; I'd always held off from going to a strip club or anything like that because I knew that I would end up feeling depressed. I remembered how it felt when the other men returned to their pints as though nothing had happened. What had been an epoch in my sad little life was an everyday thing for all of them, and that woman had given it away for free, as a joke.

What a way to finally see a pair. I hadn't got a woman home with me for a one-nighter or started a romantic relationship that had led to sexual intercourse. This was in the beer garden of a pub. They were the breasts of someone I didn't know, surrounded by loads of other people laughing about it. This was something I had always thought would be glorious, but the eventual setting had been sorrid.

The weirdest thing of all is that I couldn't remember what the breasts looked like, even thought it had been my ambition to see a pair since I was about twelve. I couldn't tell you if they were big or small or much else about them. Alcohol must have played a role—and I was drunk—but other than that, I think that my brain had been overloaded. I do remember the areola and nipples, they were about the size of a medium-sized coin and surprisingly brown. Why couldn't I remember anything else about them? I was in a prime position to get a look. I do remember the *effect* of seeing them: I didn't get an erection, but I felt it in my stomach, and I suspect, in my prostate. I have always found that to be the case when there is a "real" stimulus rather than something on a screen. No stiffy, typically, but potent biochemistry definitely at work.

When I got home it was the usual routine: stumble around, porn, wank, bed, and the next morning, a mild hangover and an opportunity to mull. As I said, the next two weeks were a bit rough. Reaching this milestone had its good and bad points. Moments of utter frustration kept welling up between times of crawling along the ground as usual. Ashes.

I thought of the times I had wished there was a service whereby guys like me could go view a pair of breasts, or even a completely naked woman, in a dignified setting. I often wondered if I could ask an acquaintance for a quick look, but I knew that was against The Rules. This was a privilege that you were either born into or had to win somehow, and no one who won was merely fat and funny.

My conclusion, at the end of the two weeks, was that my dearest wish in life was to somehow achieve a sex life. Having finally seen some boobs, I realised that they weren't, on their own, the answer to anything. A quick look wasn't enough. I sighed to myself when I realised that I was going to have to pay for sex or go beyond thirty as a virgin. Again, it was breaking The Rules a bit, but I didn't feel too bad about doing it; why shouldn't I steal a few crumbs off the table when everyone else was having a banquet?

I began to plan things out using the Internet, and eventually, I selected an attractive middle-aged woman who was based in the local area. She looked nice, but also looked like she understood what she was doing. Part of the reason that guys like me can't get laid is because we're not willing to take advantage of someone or do anything to hurt anyone. In my experience, the type of men that women adore aren't held back by the same qualms.

Then, I started making excuses. I'm good at that. I could wait until later in the year and for dark evenings because I didn't want to be seen walking into the flat that she worked out of. Financially, it was no real problem, but better to wait until I had a bit extra in my account. Not too close to a visit to Mum because she might be able to tell by looking at me. And so on, and so on.

Then mouse was announced. *What a daft, quack theory*, I had thought to myself. And then something unexpected happened.

I was calibrating a piece of test equipment in the back room of one of the chemists, and I looked over at two women who were giggling about something.

"We were talking about mouse, John," one of them said in a conspiratorial tone. "Have you heard of it?"

"Heard of it? I am on it!" I replied before adopting a mousey voice, "Squeak! I don't fancy blokes any more but it's had a few side-effects."

Much laughter, and an expression on Sarah's face that was half amusement and half annoyance.

"Well, you sarcastic sod, we know that it does work."

"Oh?"

"One of our suppliers does some defence contracts. Long story short, he told us that the Ministry of Defence discovered mouse."

"To cure homosexuality in the ranks?" I asked, now genuinely interested. There is a point in a conversation like this one at which you can be incredulous without offending the teller of the story.

"No, quite the opposite. It seems that it was going to be weaponised. But it wasn't designed to turn people straight. It was going to turn the enemy soldiers gay. The idea was to cause chaos in the middle of a war by making them fancy each other. As I said, you can't pass this on."

Her mate added, "It's true, as far as we know. Simply take a large dose of insulin, orally, and you'll start to go gay."

"If I wanted to become gay by doing this, would it be dangerous?" I asked. Clever. Putting things as bluntly as that threw them off the plan that had begun to form in my head.

"It shouldn't be, there are conditions that are treated with insulin in that way."

"That's working again," I said, pointing at the measuring machine. Did I silently wish that I could ask them both for quick look at their breasts before I left? No, because a quick look didn't fix anything and it made me feel worse. Besides, there may be no need now.

Two weeks later, the press was full of talk about reverse-mouse, confirming the story that I had been told.

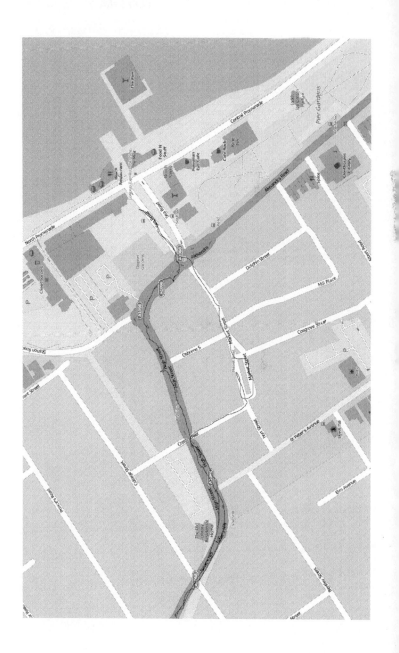

Chapter 10

The visit

"It's so easy, easy
When everybody's tryin' to please me."

My brother, Steven, has a kid, and he carries out his paternal access visits at my place. Attempting to stage the whole thing at his own flat would be laughable. For one thing, Steven is constantly surrounded by fellow druggies. For another, Steven's skills with a vacuum cleaner leave something to be desired.

I once asked him: "Do you own a vacuum cleaner?" He didn't seem sure.

I have to hand it to Susan and Steven, they cooperate to ensure that the visits run smoothly. Steven is always on time, always presentable. I don't know why that surprises me. Some people with a lifestyle like his can't cope with the implicit responsibilities of normal life, but that isn't the case with Steven. Things are easy for him, when he wants to do them.

Steven was like a wild animal that I had convinced to take food from my hand. We're not that close, but we did have a relationship that worked. Ironically, I bet there are families that are much closer and less functional than ours.

That morning, he knocked on the door, a few minutes early, as usual.

"Hey, bro!" he said before heading off for a slash.

While he was doing that, I put the kettle on and made the first mugs of tea. When Susan arrives with Tom, Steven likes to be in the lounge, PlayStation on the go. He looked up as the kid runs into the room.

Upon seeing him, Tom ran over and shouted, "Dad!"

"Watch out, you're gonna make me crash," said Steven before pausing the game and planting a kiss on the little chap. "Now, you just sit here..." before lifting the lad up onto the arm of the chair "...and we'll show your uncle John how to do it. He's a bit of a crafty one; he has more time to play it than me because I'm always out making ends meet."

Steven, what a fuck-up you are in life, and what an acceptable dad you are, given the circumstances. Ten times what you yourself had.

What does little Tom think the set up is? Children as young as him aren't as binary as adults. He accepts that this is my house, and it is his dad's house, and yet his dad lives somewhere else.

"Where do you work, Dad?" he asked once. I bet that if you added it up, he'd sometimes ask fifty questions of his idol in a typical visit.

"All over the place, son. Every hour that God sends." From the beginning, the father was instilling a work ethic in his son, thanks to the magical power of pure bullshit.

"Tom! If you're holding my arm, I can't play the game!" Steven pretended to bellow at the kid to be rewarded with a giggle. Another hour of this and then off to McDonald's for the three of us.

Susan made herself at home in the kitchen for a quick chat with me. I am fine. Work is fine. I asked her about her Uni work and it's always fascinating. I prided myself that I always had something to say in return as I read a lot of books, but I was jealous of her studies.

At one point she said, "Oh, you need to be doing this". And I supposed that she was right. Was Susan, my secret crush? Not really. My mind wouldn't go there because it shouldn't. My ideal, I suppose. Beautiful, clever and kind.

God, she's clever, and that can be intimidating because she's so young. But daft. Why does she go after someone like Steven? That's something I knew about her: Susan's type was the opposite of me.

Abruptly she said, "Right, I'm off, then. And you know what that means."

Apparently, early in our acquaintance, I had blushed when she kissed me on the cheek. Subsequently, we had to go through a teasing ritual.

"Now, I don't want you getting aroused!" she mocked. Smirking away, she gave me a bear hug, and finished with a "There you go. That was nice, wasn't it?" in a baby voice.

Like every humiliation I suffered, I had to take this one with a laugh and smile. How deliberately cruel she was being I couldn't say. Thinking about it, along with the boob lady, these experiences were the closest I had ever come to having sex with a woman.

Susan could have sex any time she liked, as much as she liked. She was one of the sexually rich. In all fairness, she had earned her position of high sexual status. Oh, wait, no she hadn't.

Why shouldn't she make fun of one of the sexually impoverished if it pleased her Ladyship? At the very least, it was not a joke between equals. It was a cruel and condescending ritual that I'd probably never be able to shake off. In addition, it had its compensations. Maybe I was getting something out of it that I wasn't supposed to; if so, good.

On this occasion, Susan had to take a trip out of town to attend a lecture that coincided with her parents going on holiday. After some discussion, we decided that Steven and I could look after the kid for one night.

After much PlayStation (tried not to thrash Steven too much in front of the kid), we took Tom up to bed. Steven had never been upstairs in my house before.

"Ah, this is pretty good, isn't it, mate? Look, you've got a tree outside the window," Steven began to tell his ever attentive son. "You're a bit too young at the moment, but in a few years time you'll go out for a pint with your old man, and we'll all stay here after the pub. But you, you'll be able to sneak back early with a chick, and then you can take her up that tree and through the window." He then adopted a conspiratorial tone. "Keep it nice and quiet. That way, me and your uncle John won't get a bollocking from yer mam." At that, he winked and Tom giggled, obviously not understanding much of what was said.

Tom had fallen asleep before his dad had finished making his daft but entertaining remarks about the room, and it occurred to me that it was Steven and I who were headed for a difficult night. I saw a fair bit of Steven, but only before, during or after a visit with Tom. Now we were tasked with spending an evening together, and basically, enjoying each other's company.

Steven tapped his fingers as we sat through a film, some of James Cameron's finest sci-fi, a film that we would have loved when we were kids. Now it was the wrong choice because he'd grown out of it. He was the childish adult and I was boring grown-up who was into childish things. He looked around and sighed, knowing better than to ask if he could have a cigarette. Steven and I got on as well as we did because we had become experts at avoiding awkwardness.

The love scene came up on screen.

"Knockers, mate. Lovely!" said Steven with a wink.

Why did I disapprove of that? I had certainly been admiring Linda Hamilton's topless scene just as much as him, probably more. I suppose I felt that it was alright to think it, but breaking the rules to say it. What a pathetic wimp I was.

Steven surprised me with a personal question, the one I dreaded. He pointed at the screen and asked,"Do you ever shag anyone?"

"Not really," I said without elaborating. And without saying, *about as often as I fight a robot from the future to protect humankind.*

"Get yerself a prozzy, mate, and get in there. I can tell you a good one."

"Right..." I said, trying to leave it at that.

So, Steven (and presumably everyone who knew me) knew that I lived a sex-free life. He also knew, somehow, that I was interested in sex. My old plan, that I had never dared to carry out, was an everyday occurrence to him. I presumed that was what he meant: that he was a frequenter of prostitutes. That was a bit surprising. As a complete arsehole to everyone, Pharaoh had constant stream of willing young women in his thrall. Yet, it seemed that he was paying for it as well. What would be enough for that guy? Then again, if it's enjoyable, why not do it, Steven? There will be practically no consequences, as it's you.

What did "get in there" mean in that context? A crude sexual point about penetration was part of what it meant. It also meant to take part in an activity, one that I should have been involved in all along as a human man. It also meant "get with the program". I'd not had a very good experience with quick fixes lately, but on the other hand, maybe one artificial success would help me to drag myself away from a sexless existence?

The conversation stopped dead at that point, and I began to feel guilty. I had implied disapproval of something that I would take part in if I had the guts. There was, however, a shade of ethical difference, as I hadn't planned to betray a current partner, as I bet Steven was always doing. Also, I only wanted to do it because I was absolutely desperate.

I was just about to attempt a light-hearted comment, when Steven could take no more. Watching *The Terminator* on a Sunday night with me was beyond what he could stand. He was as desperate to be out on the street as a tomcat in the middle of summer, so he stood up.

"Look, is it going to throw you out if I pop out for an hour or so?" He had reached for his jacket before I could reply.

I had a constitutional advantage over Steven. I was, basically, content to spend an evening in my living room, reading books and watching science fiction films, and he wasn't. It wasn't his fault that he couldn't handle a situation like that. But look at the end result. He had escaped the nine-to-five drudgery of the rat race, *and* he had an unlimited number of sexual partners. Who was the winner? Maybe it was a problem with society itself. He did everything wrong and got rewarded at every turn; I did everything right, and spent my evenings with James Cameron.

"Not at all," I said. I didn't add, *Look Steven, I'm not above going with a prostitute, and I'm sorry if I acted like I disapproved of your suggestion. In fact, I'd like any advice you could offer on the matter, as you seem to be an expert.*

Off Steven went.

"I'll leave the door unlocked. Just give it a bit of a shove," I said, knowing that I wouldn't see him before it was time for me to get up. Truth be known, I felt relieved that he was going. I did wonder where the hell he would go in an unfamiliar part of town at 10pm on a Sunday night. Not that I was worried; he'd find some fellow ne'er-do-wells to take drugs with and shag.

Chapter 11

The experiment

A few nights later, I threw a bit of jelly* in with the weekly shop. The till operator didn't suspect a thing.

You're not planning on doing something you shouldn't with this? she didn't ask when she picked it up.

Erm, no! I just fancied a bit of jelly. You know, for a change, I didn't have to reply.

On instinct, as a highly trained futuristic secret agent, I didn't lean over the side of the till to notice her holding down a little red button. Subsequently, half a dozen security guards didn't come piling out of a side-door brandishing shotguns.

You sold me out! I didn't shout at the woman.

My sudden inexplicable laughter did catch her attention though.

Careful, John. Suddenly laughing in Tesco is breaking The Rules, old man.

Telling myself to stop laughing worked, for once, and I left her to wonder what I had found so amusing about the grocery shop.

---

*jello, for Americans

I had done enough chemistry to understand what I was doing; a bit of searching around on a dodgy druggie forum on the Internet filled in the missing details. I had enough insulin to concentrate it and a put it in with some jelly, and the end result was an ice cube tray full of green jelly that I left to cool. I'd put a paper towel over it and hide it in the back of fridge later.

"Don't touch the jelly, it's gone off, I'm afraid," I practised saying to myself, as there was a slight chance that one of the lads from work might come by. On the other hand, saying: *Help yourself to the jelly, there's plenty more where that came from!* would have been expedient but unethical.

No Steven and the kid this Saturday, so I'd test it over the weekend, starting on Friday night. According to an account on the forum, within half an hour, I would feel a shift in my perception of other people, on a sexual level. The effect would apparently last well into the next day. I was surprised that I managed to sleep at all that night.

Friday morning–off to work. My first job took me to one of my regular ports of call, a large high street pharmacist.

"Hi, ladies!" I said with a grin and a wobble of eyebrows. Giggles of acknowledgement. I'm "nice" and they "like" me. I spent most of my working life interacting with women as these back-room positions in chemists tend to be a somewhat female domain. As usual, a bit of test gear wasn't reading right.

"How long before it's fixed, John?" one of the women asked me, hopefully.

I got some more giggles with: "To be honest with you: it's a quick fix. The problem is, it takes me bit longer to make sure it'll break again so that I can come back and see you all." Yes, it was a prepared line, but I had only used it twice that year.

Sorry if I looked too serious while I was working on it. I was pretending that I was a secret agent dismantling a nuclear bomb.

Typical work day over–back to the house. I had worked out two tests that I could carry out tonight. First, I planned to compare my relative reactions to gay and straight porn. Then, a quick shower and into the town for more experimentation. I'm a Saturday night man, and going out on a Friday night reduced my chances of seeing anyone I knew. Not that it would matter. It's not as though I would be tripping my head off on psychedelic drugs or anything. It wouldn't matter if I saw someone I knew while I was secretly gay. Besides, I'd go somewhere I didn't normally go, somewhere with a younger and gayer-looking crowd.

A bit of jelly, and then I forced myself to wait half an hour. No obvious effects so far. I examined the back of my hand. Certainly, something had changed in my perception of things. "Heightened" is the word I would use. But was I gay?

First the porn. I set myself up in the usual position in my bedroom and drew the curtains. As usual, I imagined an old dear gesturing towards my house and saying, "He's wanking again!"

I typed in one of the usual phrases. I'd managed to hold off on this stuff for a couple of evenings, in the interest of science.

My reaction to straight porn seemed unaffected; although, let's be honest, it's never going to induce the heart-pounding reaction that those early, grainy clips did in the 90s. This time, it was as mildly arousing, as usual.

Right, swap to gay porn. Some men would screw their faces up at the slightest suggestion of seeing homosexual sex, but it's never bothered me. It always amazed me that I was completely secure in my heterosexuality, as I know that it's an area in which most men are a bit wobbly. Y'know–men who do it with loads of women. Admittedly, at that moment, the idea of kissing a man was "icky". However, if this stuff worked, I presumed I would find the idea alluring and even arousing.

But, what now? I wondered what to type in, as I'd never

gone looking for gay porn before. In the end, the phrase "gay porn" showed a variation on the sites that I was used to. It was time to check out the scene.

I've never been that partial to a body-builder physique in men, and that was dominant in the commercial fare, it seemed. On the other hand, I didn't think I'd want to look at a splodge like myself. Typing in "amateur gay porn" produced some better results. I spotted a few of the aforementioned splodge type bodies in the thumbnails, and then, a nice looking young British couple going at it. Ordinary looking, but "fit", in both senses of the word.

All in all, it was the type of scene that I usually go for: natural bodies and an obviously amateur shoot. Realism is what I like. The two guys both looked mischievous. For porn to work, it has to break some rules, and what was going on in this scene was that the two guys were obviously a real couple. That was the line that was being crossed: seeing a couple in a private moment.

They sucked, they wanked, they fucked a bit. Still, it didn't really do it for me. They had the camera balanced on a surface just beyond the bed. At one point, most of what I could see was the foot of one of the men. Not particularly appealing. That was odd. I'm not a foot fetishist, but I've often liked seeing a woman's bare foot in a scene like this. How would I feel if that man's foot were thrust into my hand? Ugh.

I tried to masturbate a little, and I've no doubt that I could have let nature take its course, but equally, I could have got myself off looking at a blank wall, if I had to.

It hadn't worked. And yet, things *did* feel different. There was a possible explanation. Sexuality must be formed over the course of a lifetime, and I hadn't reacted to this stimulus because I had no precedents. For example, let's say I had a crush on a girl when I was ten. Perhaps that, along with millions of other relatively insignificant events, shaped what I was into, sexually.

Something was definitely different, though, I was sure of that.

Time for part two of the experiment.

Getting dressed presented a question: what should I wear? I have absolutely no sense of style and a short-sleeved button-up shirt along with my brown leather jacket is my usual choice. Should I dress gay? As part of the clear-out from a late relative that I had never met, I had inherited a few items that were outside my usual drab style. If my body has an attractive attribute, and I'm not arguing that it does, I have fairly thick arms. I selected a red t-shirt with gold fleck.

Thanks, uncle whoever-you-were.

As luck would have it, I also had some white jeans that I had bought on a whim and regretted. Then, the Brylcreem! Where the hell had that come from? From when I lived at home, obviously, but why had I brought it with me? It must be at least fifteen years old by now. I went into the bathroom to give it a little sniff. It seemed all right. I tried not to use too much and gave myself a side-parting for a change.

Whether talking about web design or painting and decorating, the trick is to keep things as simple as possible when dabbling in an unfamiliar field. Until then, that had been my policy with dress. Checking myself out in the mirror, I looked like someone making a bit of a statement rather than someone who wanted to disappear. I looked like I might be gay without looking daft.

Feeling a bit precocious, I added a condom to the condom pouch of my wallet. It was the first time it had contained one. I knew that the condom was still good, as I had refreshed the packet earlier in the year, surreptitiously, while I was out of town. I'd bought a quite a few over the years, each time a somewhat sad duty. Occasionally, I had got one out for a look and a play around with, but mostly, they went out of date. I wrapped them up when throwing them up, so that they wouldn't be seen by the bin men.

A couple of years earlier, that twat Steven had needed some of my condoms.

"Not got any johnnies, have you?" he asked me after tapping on my door at 1am.

"Erm... yep." Why did I pause, as though having to

think about it? Was I implying that I was using them at such a rate that I couldn't reliably recall if I had any left? More likely, I had hinted at the truth, that once they were bought, they were shoved into the sock drawer to lie untouched.

"I couldn't borrow a couple, could I?" he asked.

"Borrow them? Okay, but you better give them a damn good wipe afterwards," I said, as I headed upstairs.

"Champion, mate!"

Upon my return, I threw him the box. "Might as well take the lot. There's every chance I won't be getting laid tonight."

"Good lad." He took them over to the standard lamp to examine them.

"They're extra small. I hope that's acceptable."

"No, it's not that," he replied. "Just checking that they're still good." He had the decency to smile with embarrassment at that one.

Oh well, at least they would get some use. His sex life was a bit hectic. The bastard. He'd lie and cheat on whoever the latest one was, and his older brother had never been able to get a girlfriend or have sex.

It wasn't just the number of women he got, it was the type of women he got. It would have seemed reasonable that he'd wake up next to another druggie from time to time, given his lifestyle, but that isn't what Steven liked. And Steven got whatever he liked in life. Steven had girlfriends rather than one night stands. Not being University educated was a rarity and the relationships went on for months. How did they put up with him? Why did they put up with him? They became exasperated with him, but never truly angry. That's because it was never truly his fault, in their eyes. It always seemed to me that it was *their* fault for putting themselves through the mill with him. It might have been that the women got something out of it that I couldn't figure out?

Chapter 12

A gay night out

"A brave man dies once, a coward a thousand times."

I gave the house a last look around. Ever the optimist, I had tidied up, just in case.

Wallet, keys, phone. Wallet, keys, phone.

I normally wore a watch, but watches are for sensible people.

Goodbye, house. Goodbye, old me.

May fortune favour the foolish.

I decided to walk all the way into town to give myself a bit of practice and to get into character. I had never before felt like I did that night. For one thing, I felt purposeful. I was a man on a mission and I swaggered as I walked. I felt like I had been holding my stomach in since puberty. And now, I was letting it all hang out. I was on the pull, frankly. Starting at thirty when it came to sex? No big deal. A lot of gay people had a late start on their sex life. In the straight world, women rated me as a three out of ten. I felt sure that I'd do much better as a gay man.

After fifteen minutes of walking (and swaggering), I reached the corner that led into town. 10pm was a good starting time for a night of clubbing in Cleethorpes. There are probably about fifteen little clubs, all open until the early hours. I had never been in any of them. In the past, I had danced a little, down the pub, when extremely drunk, usually on my own and for the amusement of the lads. How humiliating for me.

As I rounded the corner, my swagger missed a beat as I saw a police car parked outside of a club. Weird. What was I doing wrong? Okay, I stole some chemicals. The truth is that I was going equipped for homosexuality, and instinctively, I thought it might have showed. I smirked to myself at my private joke. But this raised a question: did gay people like a joker? Heterosexual women didn't seem to find it very attractive.

A typical night out would consist of me standing with guys I knew vaguely from work while holding my pint at my chest. There are areas for men like me in every club and every pub that has a dance floor. They should be clearly marked: "Sad Lonely Bastard Zone", and then the small print: "This area is for sad bastards who can't get anyone to dance with them. Old geezers who are just out for a perv are also allowed to use this area. No dancing other than vaguely nodding and moving a leg in time to the music."

This time it was going to be different.

Frankly, I presumed that the sexual negotiations would be a bit simpler with other men. Some might say that my assumption was based on a stereotype about gay people, but I was sure that it wouldn't be endless rounds of game-playing, posturing and proving of one's worth.

As I walked along the street, someone doing promo for a club handed me a flyer for a free shot with my first drink. I knew the upstairs of that one to be decidedly fruity, but when I went in, I began with two drinks in the downstairs bar before venturing up.

Okay, I thought, *let's see what this baby can do.*

Once at the top of stairs, sure enough, lots of young men with tight t-shirts were laughing and hugging each other. I had pulled into Gayville, it seemed. Good.

Here was a question: did they know that I might be gay? I had gaydar, but was I throwing out a gay signature that thcy could detect? Sure enough, I got a few looks back. It was working!

After a couple more drinks, I prepared to continue with this phase of the experiment. Even standing there, sambuca in hand, the situation was different from the usual one. I *was* standing with my drink, observing as usual, but this time I was checking out the lie of the place while concocting an overall strategy for the evening.

I usually planned my drinking to be nicely drunk by home time. What a boring fellow I had been. What a sad time of the night home time was. Sometimes, I'd have a go at drunkenly joking around with the staff as they were packing up, to stave off the inevitable. It's probably just as well that I wasn't born a woman as God knows what I'd do to avoid going home by myself.

With pretend confidence that had been enhanced by alcohol, I walked towards the dance floor, for once, with intent. I found a pillar, and I stood next to it while surveying the scene. Damn it, those are the standing places for losers! I'd use it to get my bearings and then launch off in my new persona as a homosexual club-monkey.

Through a fractal on a breaking wall, I pushed off and soon stood two metres away from the safety of the pillar. I had an Ace up my sleeve as, earlier in the week, I had looked up "dancing in clubs" on YouTube. Let's just say, I now knew a few moves. Casually, I employed the *step touch*, one of the dances I had practised in front of the laptop. It worked a bit, but I think I must have learned the wrong dance for this type of music. It was very hard to do the *step touch* fast enough. I looked around. No one else was doing the *step touch*. It was probably a good dance move, but it was too complicated.

I simplified things, movement-wise, and bopped along on pure instinct, persevering for the rest of the song and then headed back to the bar. After a sambuca and then one more sambuca, my thinking became clearer. Back on the dance floor, and things went a bit seventies. Thank God the DJ seemed to have his head screwed on, finally.

"Freak Out!" indeed. Standing on my own, I had a considerable groove going on, and I kept it up for a couple of songs. What an enjoyable sensation, but why not seize upon this run of good luck, groove-wise?

I spotted a likely target of a few lads dancing together. Before I had a chance to reconsider, I pushed off towards them.

"I want to dance with all of you!" I exclaimed. Communication in a club can be a bit hit and miss, but they all heard what I said and began to laugh. One of the guys beckoned me and I was suddenly in their circle. I wondered what the reaction would have been if I'd tried that with a bunch of women back when I was straight. My guess, either a disgusted shake of the head or simply, "Fuck off, mate!"

No explanations are needed when you are young, gay and slamming the fuck out of the dance floor. Sometimes I danced as part of the group and other times I homed in on an individual to welcoming laughs and smiles that I hoped were well meant. Then again, who cares?

Looking at one guy, I wondered what it would be like to have casual sex with him. No real feelings of note seemed to be cropping up. I felt sure that I was changed by the mouse, but that once again, the problem was a lack of context. I hadn't grown up fancying men and I had no specific ideas about what I liked. Big muscles? Not really. The guy in front of me had a nice face and a trim body. Not bad.

Would I be into a fellow fat blokes, if I met one I liked? When I fancied women, I liked a full figure, but even then, what context did I have? About half the time, I clicked on thumbnails featuring women who looked like housewives, complete with flabby bodies. Older women's bodies always looked characterful, and basically, hot, to me. However, if I got close to such a woman, touched her, and got a proper look, would I like it as much as I did on screen? If everyone liked it, why weren't middle-aged women with love-handles on the cover of every magazine and being used to sell products? Furthermore, if no one else liked

it, could I really like it as much as I thought I did? But
that was crazy talk; if no one else *did* like it, why did
housewifey women on porn sites get voted up with tons
of appreciative comments underneath? Certainly, part of
the appeal was getting a look at someone I shouldn't be
seeing naked.

I looked around and my new friends had disappeared.
Ah, that's life in the fast lane of clubland. Stumbling
around, I decided to try another club while still gay.

Next up, a club called Rio. I nodded to the bouncers
and they were quick to acknowledge me and wave me in.
They knew a man in a hurry when they saw one. Once
inside, I paid my money and strolled in to the main area.
To think, I'd lived here my whole life and been content to
simply wonder what it was like inside.

The club was fairly packed and there was some classic
rock playing. First problem encountered. I absolutely
love Queen, my first CD was a Queen CD, but was I still
into Queen? As great as Queen are, as a band, they are
what a boring bloke down the pub likes. I decided to be
honest about my feelings. I'd enjoy it and it would be nice
to have something familiar while I took stock of the place
and formulated my plans. Besides, I felt worrying pangs
of soberness beginning to take hold; I judged that some
red sambuca could solve that problem. I supped at the
little plastic cup and surveyed the place from the vantage
point of the bar. Erk—there were straight people of my
own age group everywhere. However, I had paid to get in,
so I decided to wander around.

I briefly considered buying a pint just to have something
to hold, but that was boring bloke thinking. I didn't want
a comforter to help me fit in and disappear. I wanted
to be able to hit that dance floor at a second's notice
when I needed to. Besides, I get drunk rather quickly
for a fat bloke, and I had lost count of how many red
sambucas I had sloshed down so far. I wobbled a bit
when I pushed off from the bar. Oh well, maybe a man
would spot my vulnerability and decide to take advantage.
Hmm... When I was a straight guy, a woman doing that

would have been my dream come true, but even drunk and mousing it, the opposite didn't seem as appealing. I decided to be on my guard, but still open to whatever homosexual possibilities presented themselves in this place.

As luck would have it, the floor plan was arranged in a figure eight with two separate dance floors, and things improved a bit as I moved onto the dancier dance floor. As I walked around the corner, Madonna came on. Express myself? Yes, that's what I'm trying to do, Madonna! At least it wasn't *Like A Virgin*. Even Madonna was on my side and egging me on that night. I tried to stumble around as expressively as possible and had a go at expressing myself at the corner at the dance floor. I attracted some confused stares from women. This place just wasn't gay enough for a guy like me.

I began to feel as though I had overdone things as I flounced around. Damn it, I was at optimum performance for a while there. I'd accomplished a lot on my first expedition. Time to cut my losses and head back to base.

"Mouse you later!" I shouted to a gaggle of women and topped it off with a salute. They must have been foreign or something and they didn't understand me.

By that time, I was beginning to feel groggy, but that was probably a side effect of the mouse, I reasoned. I pushed off and tried to maintain my balance. I always feel like I'm The Terminator when I'm as drunk as this. I was reduced to basics. *Move forward. Recall mission parameters. Someone approaching. Carry out threat assessment. No threat detected. Locate building exit from memory bank. Plot safe route. Hold on to pillar. Proceed to exit. Nod to concerned doorman. Proceed out of building. Continue onto main road. Plot optimal route.*

By the time I was near my street, I realised that I had a choice. I could bolt down an alley and throw up now, or I could baby myself back to the house, and perhaps, not vomit. Choosing the latter over the former, I set off down the road. A few minutes later, I quietly unlocked the door and walked into the house without rushing things.

I whispered: "God of Booze, I have been taught enough of a lesson. Yes, I drank way too much, but I accept that fact, and any further lesson would be superfluous. Besides, I have lot on my mind at the moment, and it's perfectly understandable that I have overdone things."

My excuse-making, coupled with a lack of a truly penitent attitude, angered The God of Booze. Teenage experience told me not to run. Solemnly, I proceeded into the bathroom and chucked up. What a night.

Chapter 13

Straightening things out

Sometimes you have to strike when the iron's hot. It's called momentum, and I seemed to have built some up. I didn't know where I was headed exactly, but you get to a point where life is so steady that you're sick of being comfortable.

"Y'know, I'm a bit sick of the way you make fun of me when you're ready to go," I said to myself. It was a good opening, truthful and direct. "I'm not much of a sexual success, and I'm sick of you lording it over me," I continued, practising what I was going to say to Susan.

"Tell me, Susan, what did you do to earn your success in that area of life?" That would be sticking it to her. A few home truths. No losing my nerve and apologising to her. This would be a bitter pill that would take a while to have its full effect. Let her leave angry or even storm out. She'd have to come back eventually, and when she did, we'd be on a much better footing. I have been a joker, but I am not a joke. How about adding, "You mean a lot to me, Susan" to the beginning of it? Somehow I knew that starting off like that would put me in control.

Once we were in the kitchen, Susan started on about things in the usual way. It was difficult to cut in; I had to make it seem natural. Plain words were the best way to get started, and then back to what I had prepared.

"There is something I want to say," I said, suddenly.

"Oh, right? Sounds serious."

I didn't want to do it. Who cares if she made fun of me a bit? I vaguely remembered promising myself that I would persevere. It was important for some reason that I couldn't remember. Besides, I had to say something now. Go on John, blurt it out!

I blurted: "I'm sick of the way you make fun of me. I'm a virgin and it's not my fault."

"Oh, um," she mumbled before laughing and biting her upper lip in an attempt to stop.

I was glad she was laughing. It gave me the courage to finish off the job.

"It's pretty funny for you, Susan, because everything goes your way when it comes to sex. You're a nice looking woman and you've got big tits, and I wonder how I ended up being a complete bloody joke around here!"

I kept my voice down, and I'd shut the intervening doors for the sake of Steven and the kid. This was proper grown-up stuff, and I had impressed myself. It was like a row in *Coronation Street*.

That said, it was, maybe, a bit stronger than I had meant. Oh, and what had I told her? I'd handed over my most humiliating secret to someone whom I'd just made an enemy of. Now I was even more of a joke. Oh, for a time machine.

"Okay..." She then had to stifle her laughter again. So much for not being a joke any more. Why did I feel like I had just transitioned from nervously standing on the side of the road to putting myself into the middle of the road, with heaving traffic bearing down on me? She put her hand in front of her mouth and then touched me on the shoulder. This is why people never fix things, because it feels crap.

To make matters worse, I felt guilty because she is dependent on me for the visits. Now I was leveraging that position to berate her over something not very important.

What an arsehole. I would have been better off saying, "Oh, I'm not playing that any more" and pulling away from her next time she started up. That would have done the job. She would have made a joke about me being touchy. It might have taken a few goes but it would have worked eventually. Anything was better than this.

Then she ramped things up by locking eyes with me and said, "I'm sorry..." and then she pretended to start crying. That did it. Susan was making things a lot easier for me by keeping me angry with her. And... I realised that she *was* crying. Her apology was obviously genuine too. On the positive side, this wasn't going to turn into a screaming match.

Steven burst into the room.

"I just need a..." he began.

"We're in the middle of something, Steven," she said. "Out!"

He obeyed.

"I am sorry, John. I didn't mean to make fun of you." We both stood there quietly for a while as she continued to sniffle.

After a while, I sighed and told her it didn't matter that much.

"It does matter, and I shouldn't have done it."

I'd uncorked the bottle, and as a result, I felt shivery but no longer angry. Another pause and more sniffling from her while she looked at the floor.

God, this must be what it feels like to have a girlfriend. Perhaps it isn't worth it.

I wondered if getting a boyfriend was going to be free from moments like this.

"Why are you crying?" I asked, breaking the sniffly silence. This was followed by another pause that once again made me feel as though being girlfriendless over the course of my entire life had an upside to it.

"I seem to turn everyone against myself. Usually by ripping the piss out of them. Especially of late. I am sorry," she said.

"It's really okay. It's a bit of a sore subject for me, as

you can imagine. I've been going through a lot recently, and I'm trying to get things sorted out."

Although I felt as though I had been balancing on a high-wire recently, summarising things out loud had helped. Now that the problem wasn't unmentionable, it didn't seem insurmountable.

Susan put her hand on my shoulder and said, "I'm sorry things don't work out for you, in that area. It's unfair."

I don't think it was conceited to feel that I hadn't humiliated myself at all. The truth of the matter is that I'm not the worst guy in the world, and I didn't deserve to be in the bottom five percent of all thirty-year-old men when it came to sexual success. It *was* unfair.

"I've got to go now, John," she said. Then she gave me a lovely hug followed up by a smile. That was a bit better.

After everyone had left, I started putting some of my clothes into bin bags, ready to be thrown out. I had considered donating them to a charity shop, but I didn't want to pass on the curse that I had been living under to some other hapless sod in search of a bargain.

I went through every item in my wardrobe and chest of drawers in turn and asked myself, honestly, if they made me feel happy or sad. Never mind if they were still perfectly good. The money didn't matter, and if I could make a few improvements to my life, that was a bargain in itself. I bet to myself that I'd end up regretting this when I was in a steadier state of mind. Tough. When you're on a roll, you have to make the most of it. I was sure I'd be back to excuse-making soon enough. The new me was going to make some improvements, and the old me would be the beneficiary, if I ever went back to what I used to be.

Why had I put up with horrible shirts that I hated? I must have secretly hated myself. The brown leather jacket was a tough one, relatively valuable and functional as it was. It was incredibly straight, and very much the garment of a boring individual.

"For a man with no ideas!" the catalogue should have said. "Boring bloke down the pub? Then this is for you!"

I considered a ceremonial cremation for it in the back yard, but it seemed like too much trouble. Quick check of the pockets, and in the bin bag it went. Most of my clothes followed it.

Before long, I had some bags piled up in the hallway. The bag with the jacket, however, was already in the wheely bin and ready to go. I had done this to stave off the temptation to retrieve it. Not everything I now had left over was absolutely awful, and I had just enough apparel to get me through the week. How different I felt, sitting in my living room with a blue shirt and black trousers, looking reasonably smart. What a different view on life.

I popped my head around the door at the hairdressers.

"Do I need an appointment?" I asked.

"No, we can fit you in in five minutes."

As I sat there, I looked at the three women who were working. I'd I had taken a bit of jelly this morning, so my interest was dulled, but being objective about it, they were all gorgeous. Hairdressers tended to be, I had noticed. I suppose you have to look attractive when you're selling a service that makes people more attractive. After five minutes, a chair freed up and one of the girls indicated to me.

"Now, I've got a challenge for you," I said as I sat down.

"Really?"

"I'd like you to make me look absolutely gorgeous, to both men and women. But, as you're not a magician or a plastic surgeon, can you do anything with this?" I pointed at my head. Now, that was some good banter and it earned some laughs.

"Erm, I'll see what I can do," she said with another smile. "Who's your normal hairdresser?"

"My mum." That one didn't need any delivery to get a good laugh.

"What are you after?" she asked, good-naturedly.

"Something a bit trendy. I want to go clubbing. This is boring," I pointed at the mum-special again.

Something occurred to me. I love women. I love being around them and talking to them. I get on with them much better than I do with men. Sex had been getting in the way until now for two reasons. Firstly, because I had a desperation about me that was obvious. Secondly, because they all found me as sexually alluring as something that they had just trodden on.

Freed up from the whole sex thing, I suddenly wanted to get to know some more women. Usually, they regarded me as either below their contempt or as a complete clown. I was going to change that by being myself rather than having a "please, please, please, like me" act. I had an Ace up my sleeve. I love making people laugh, and surprisingly for a boring bloke, I have the knack. With women more than men, for some reason.

I checked out the hairdo in the mirror, and it was exactly what I'd asked for. I'm British and I would have said I liked it anyway, but it was brilliant. She'd been a bit aggressive, and maybe taken some liberties, but she knew her stuff. At the very least, I looked more like I was in the "twenty five to thirty" than the "thirty to thirty five" age group.

"That is exactly what I wanted," I told her in all honesty. She knew.

I had been invisible to the local youths for a long time; they weren't interested in engaging with a boring grown-up bloke. However, as I was leaving the barbers, two such specimens slowed down in their noisy, blinged-out saloon. One of the tracksuit-clad little bastards leaned out of the window and enquired of me, "Aww... Get yer hair cut, y'poofter?" before cackling and speeding off.

Mission accomplished, I thought to myself happily. I was back in the game, in so many ways, of late.

Chapter 14

The next week

According to the dodgy forum, there were a few methods of extracting insulin from over-the-counter medicines. I made a note of what I needed, and I decided to start buying things before they became widely known as sources of insulin. I thought about all the other people who must be going through the same process as me. I wondered if, eventually, I would be able to get what I needed off the National Health Service? Sexual reassignment was available, so maybe sexual *orientation* reassignment would be free one day? I had been miserable as a straight man, and I had not been able to form a single sexual relationship by the time I was thirty years old. Surely, that would meet the criteria for assistance?

That week, I turned my attention to the problem of refilling my wardrobe. I didn't want to go mad on that front, in part because I didn't know what I wanted. I hate buying new things because, about half the time, I end up going off it by the time I get it home. Besides, I had a feeling I was at the start of a journey that would involve a few changes along the way. A couple of non-horrible work shirts and some new trousers were a good start.

In that vein, I paid a visit to a shop that looked appropriate. After long deliberations that had led to the selection of some plain shirts, I looked around for something that would suit a fast-paced social scene. It was agonising. A t-shirt made out of silvery material looked good, but it also looked a bit ridiculous.

There should be a chain of shops called *I'm Clueless,* for guys like me. I'd pay an extra twenty-five percent for good advice, preferably from a team of experts who were certified sexual successes. If I was running it, *things that look quite good,* would be the first floor, so that idiots like me can buy clothes. *Things that look like they cost about ten pounds, things that look like they cost about thirty pounds* and *things that look like they cost about fifty pounds* would be the other floors, and they would be for buying presents.

I spotted a shop assistant, and although he didn't look gay, he did look like he knew his way around a club.

"Hiya, mate," I ventured. "I'm looking for a bit of advice."

"What about?" the good-looking person asked me, making me instantly realise that I had made a mistake.

Oh, I'm thinking of buying a new car, I didn't say. *So, I decided to come to this clothing shop to get some advice and buy one from you.*

I did pause though. I decided to *say something*.

"Clothing, of course. It's a clothes shop, right?" I said, with a puzzled expression. What was he going to do, beat me up for being impertinent?

I'm not as good-looking as you, but I danced with some homosexuals in a club last Friday.

"Right... what sort of advice do you want, though?" A reasonable question, I supposed.

"I'm just looking for some new going out things. What's hot at the moment?" I said with a cheery grin.

"It's just what you can see," he said, sweeping his hand around the entire shop.

"Right... "

"Let me know if you need anything," he added and then walked off.

Oh I will. I WILL! I didn't exclaim before falling to my knees and grabbing his calves.

Thank you. Thank you. Thank you. I didn't squeal with star-struck admiration at Good-Looking Guy.

You are the wind beneath my wings, you little cock-knocker, I didn't say before getting the big silver gun out of my pocket.

Oh, and here's something else for you. We'll call it a little extra to thank you for all your help, I would have been well within my rights to add before opening fire.

I considered dropping the shirts I had already chosen on the ground and walking out, but it had taken me so long to choose them that I decided to buy what I had already picked out. It meant giving the shop some of my money, even though they employed my nemesis, this Antichrist.

The nob-end was watching me when I went to the till. *Oh, of course, he's not working on the till; it would be beneath someone of his talents.* He stretched a little as he stood there. It was obviously his job to be a good-looking guy who stands around in a clothes shop and is completely useless. As I stood waiting to pay, I wondered what the job interview consisted of.

So basically, it will be your job to be good-looking and stand around in the shop. You'll have to be able to yawn occasionally.

Will I have to know about the stock?

No, it's very important that you don't know anything about the shop or anything that we sell. Unless it's a good-looking woman you're talking to, of course. Then you can try be helpful. It won't matter if you're not. You are good-looking, after all.

So, the job is standing around and being a good-looking, unhelpful nob-*end?*

That's it!

Will I be able to chat up the good-looking co-workers, who'll think that I'm great and that my crap jokes are funny because I'm so good-looking?

I'm afraid we're going to have to insist you do that.

When can I start?

At first, I liked the extra attention that my new look was getting me at work. By Friday, I was sick of it. On my first couple of calls on Monday, the new hairstyle and smarter clothes had drawn some comments.

"Ooh, look at the new hairdo" said one of the lab-techs before reaching over and giving it a tussle. "Someone must have a girlfriend, I think," said another. I was thirty, not fifteen! I might be giving out some gay vibes now, but until recently, I was a sexually interested heterosexual man, and these were women. Don't get me wrong, I'm not saying that I was only interested in one thing. I was happy to engage with these women as friends, but not as their young nephew. Getting out of the game had given me an objective view of what my situation had been, and I concluded that it had been half my own fault. By the middle of the week, I started to give a polite smile of acknowledgement when the hair or the clothes were commented on. From now on, I decided, no more clowning around, lest I be thought a clown.

Some of the women treated me with a bit of respect. Erica was chatting about her degree with a co-worker.

"I'm thinking of doing an Open University degree," I mentioned to her.

"Oh really? I'm doing chemistry and biology for work." I knew her a bit better than some of the others because her husband was the manager at a different pharmacist and I knew him. "What are you going to take?"

"I haven't decided yet," I replied. "I've only just started thinking about doing it."

"Is it for career, or just out of interest?"

"Maybe a bit of both. Something technical would be the obvious choice for me, and as you say, that would help me career-wise. But, it's tempting to do something just because it's fascinating. My sister-in-law is doing anthropology and politics, and that really does seem interesting."

"As I said, I'm just doing it for the job," she said. "I want more money! I'm a bit surprised that you say anthropology. And I don't mean any offence by that; I'm sure you'd be clever enough."

"None taken. The truth is–and this sounds big-headed– if I took something technical, to do with the job, then I'd probably find it really easy. In addition, as you say, it could lead to more money. However..."

She nodded. She knew exactly what I was saying. "Don't have a family, John. I love my family, but I wish I was stuck with a dilemma like yours. It wouldn't have hurt anything to have the kids ten years later than we did. I'd do english lit. or history or something like that, if I could study what I wanted."

What a difference. I do have the knack for making people laugh, but I'd relied on it far too much. I felt embittered about my status, or lack of it, with the women, but it was becoming clear to me that I had played a hand in what had happened to me.

Joan, a kindly sixty-year-old dispensary tech engaged me in a different way while I was on another maintenance call. In the past, I'd looked at her and thought, *I wonder if she would have sex with me if I had some way of asking her?* I felt guilty about it, but the truth was, I reasoned, a sixty-year-old ought to be grateful for a chance of sex with a thirty-year-old. What a horrible way to reduce sexual courtship to the level of horse-trading. However, I wonder if a sixty-year-old single man would be offended by such an offer from a thirty-year-old woman? Bit different then, eh? I felt bad, as though I had been putting Joan down, in my thoughts. And the truth is, back when I was interested, I would much rather have done it with someone like her, who I liked, than with the booby lady from down the pub, for example.

At first I thought it was going to be the type of condescending comment that I had been getting since the beginning of the week.

"Someone looks a bit different," she began.

I nodded and smiled to acknowledge what she had said.

I didn't make a daft joke about it.

"But the question is, does this represent a change from within?" she said with a wry grin.

How did she know? What did she know?

I answered her as honestly as I could. "I am trying to change a few things. Bit fed up with the old me."

"When you're as ancient as I am, you realise that when you want to change things, you should just do it. You can't see that when you're young, but it's true."

It was a thought that I carried around with me for the rest of the week.

It had been an interesting week, but the whole thing had been leading up to Friday night. I didn't want a repeat of last Friday's vomity end to the evening, so a hearty meal was the order of the day once I got home. I settled on some pasta with tuna, a safe choice. I left that bubbling away in the kitchen and put in some time with a dance instruction video on YouTube. The *step touch* had failed to set the dance floor on fire as I had hoped, but I'd been switching between various styles over the course of the week. Getting into the groove along with the combined effect of mouse and loads of alcohol seemed to be the formula. I was going to stick with what (sort of) worked.

Earlier in the week, I had joined a dating site, but I hadn't dared add a profile for myself, at least not yet. I had begun by searching for gay men within a file five mile radius to see what was on offer. As I looked down the gallery, I felt myself shifting in my seat. Here I was, sober and eyeing up some potential men. The same problem that I had run into all along had cropped up: I had no context to put all of this in, no history with it. I had an idea of what I had been looking for in a woman, but what sort of guys was I into?

As they stared into the camera, it was as though they were staring at me. When I was straight and looking at women, I didn't feel like this, but I had long ago given up on trying to create sparks; I had become convinced that I didn't stand a chance. I wondered if I could have provoked a feeling like this by being more proactive with women.

I don't know what I had expected from this side of the site, something more overtly sexual, I suppose. There were a few women on the "men seeking men" area, and they must have filled in the profile incorrectly. They were women rather than cross-dressing men, I would say. I bet they all wondered why men kept in-boxing them to tell them they looked extremely convincing.

Overall, the men looked like a nice bunch of average blokes. I'd say about one in twelve was actively trying to look effeminate or camp. I hopped over to "men looking for women" to look for differences between the gay and heterosexual guys on the site. By comparison, the gay guys certainly knew how to present themselves. To begin with, on the whole, they were smartly turned out, even though they were casually dressed. There didn't seem to be many bodybuilders around, but it looked like everyone worked out. Even the chubbier blokes looked like they were toned. The older ones had embraced youthfulness.

What a frump I felt. And how arrogant. What a lack of effort I had made in that area over the last ten years or so. I resolved to buy some weights. The slightest improvement in that area would be worth it. Again, it would function as a symbol. The gay men on the site seemed to be making the best of things with their body and their clothes. It wasn't vanity; they were sending out the proper signals. For most of my life, I had sent out signals that I was a fat, boring bloke who expected people to guess what I was I like underneath. It was equivalent to turning up for a job interview without having shaved or without bothering to wear a suit. As I straight man, I hadn't been playing the game at all.

The posing of the photographs was interesting. Usually with an arm around a friend, maybe lifting a pint towards whoever was taking the photo. I hadn't put a profile up yet, but I bet that if I had, it would have featured a photo of myself with a neutral expression, standing against a wall.

I had been on the site in the past, as a straight man, not to advertise but to peer out from my hiding place. Like it or not, gay or straight, a man was expected to show that he was taking an active rather than passive role in courtship. Oh, if only the straight world were different.

I still felt that women had never given me a chance, and that I would have preferred the female role in courtship. How many women do you know who would not be able to get laid if their life depended on it? That was the source of my bitterness. I was sure that I had been treated unfairly by women who worshipped arseholes, but what had I expected, exactly? That I would stand there, make no effort, not initiate anything, and yet be a sexual success with the women? We can't all be Tom Cruise or Ronnie Cray. I had given it zero percent effort and achieved zero success. As a gay guy, I wasn't going to make the same mistake. This time around, I was going to at least try.

What did a gay man want? My expectations had been mired in cliché and were considerably off the mark. I had expected this part of the site to be a meat market, just because the people were gay. I clicked on some profiles. "Looking for a mate" said one. And another. This was getting better. What a great starting point, to be looking for someone to be friends with. I had long suspected that was a large part of being gay. A mate that you could discuss James Bond and cameras with before heading upstairs for a bit of sex!

I flicked back to "women seeking men" for a moment. On the whole, it was a different story from the profiles that I had just been looking at. Many of the women's ads began by telling the reader off in the first line, if not in the title itself. "Sick of liars" or "Are there any good men around?" were common ones. One woman had cut and pasted a picture of a list that specified what makes a good boyfriend. These cropped up quite often. None of the adverts (by men or by women) contained a list of what was wrong with the typical woman or what the expectations of a good girlfriend should be. This particular Facebook-fodder list, in amongst the requirements for the man to be supportive and always take her side, specified that the man should always be willing to lend her money if she needed it.

Sometimes, the telling off was a warning that a prospective male shouldn't be after sex. Amusingly, a large proportion of the ones telling men that they needn't expect a one-night-stand were accompanied by saucy, down-blouse selfies of the woman. I was looking at this scene through very different eyes, now that I was an outsider. I would have estimated some of them to be at about the same attractiveness level as myself, but it was clear that they had never had to get the hang of being nice to people. Many of them came across as fat, miserable and aggressive. And yet, they were calling the shots.

About fifty percent of the women's ads were what I would call "nasty", but they weren't all like that. In fact, a lot of them were charming and respectful. I wondered why I hadn't picked up on these differences when I was interested in women. That said, flipping back to the gay side of the site, it looked more like a dating scene that I could get along with. It was what I had been looking for, in slightly different packaging, my whole life. Was it the sexual free-for-all that I had expected? No. A world that I could see myself fitting into? It looked like it could be.

Having eaten, a shower and a shave later, I was ready to hit the street. It was a bit chilly, so the smart trousers and the same shirt as last week were complemented with my best black jacket. Not getting dressed up to go out at the weekend now seemed unacceptable; how things had changed over the course of a week. I hope I looked good, but at the very least, I had adhered to symbols and customs to show my intent. At least I was trying, and I looked like me on a good day, for once. I was sure that men would give me a chance. You didn't have to be a superbly masculine winner in life to impress other men, I felt.

The changes I had made were easy. Mouse had made

me brave. I always felt that I had been treated badly, or at the very least that I had been underrated by the opposite sex. However, it was only fifty percent of the equation. I had lacked the bravery to make an effort on my own behalf. It takes a lot of courage to be yourself. Yes, I'd been a coward, and no, there was no excuse for that.

My look was gay-lite, I wasn't going to camp things up too much. There was no denying that mouse had an effect on me, though. In the first week of it, I think that I imagined myself as a camp party lad, but that wasn't the sort of gay man I wanted to be, or could ever be. Back in the playground, being gay had meant sticking one's hand out and making the teapot sign. I remember seeing an episode of *The Ellen Show* in which a lad was given the opportunity to tell Madonna that he came out to his family by dancing to one of her songs. This raises the question: what does dancing to a Madonna song have to do with being a homosexual?

The "gay community" wanted it both ways. Half the time, being gay meant you were like Graham Norton, but when it suited them, gay people were just like everyone else. And yet, for so many prominent gay men, even gay activists, being gay influenced their personality. Maybe that's what camp is? It's what happens when a man doesn't have to win female approval. I no longer cared about that stuff. For me, all controls were set to zero, and I was finding out what sort of man I wanted to be. Something had gone wrong in society, people had allowed debates about sexual role to become the purview of gay people. Everyone should be involved in it, and I wished I had been before now.

One of the lads from work had asked if I'd be down the pub on Saturday, but I blew him off.

"Family stuff," I told him.

I've made myself gay, chemically, I didn't tell him. *I'll almost certainly be too hung over on Saturday morning,*

*and besides, with a bit of luck, I'll be waking up next
to some bloke I've just shagged. Then I'll have shagged
someone and be a fully sexual being, at last.*

Maybe, in time, I could learn to straddle both worlds,
but for the moment, holding a pint at chest height in a
beer garden didn't hold any interest for me. How could
it ever have done? The biggest thrill for me in the last
few years? Seeing a woman's mammary glands. Now I'd
be about as interested in seeing her elbows, and that had
freed me, as so many aspects of being gay had. What had
constituted the humiliation that defined my character and
made me, ironically, the human equivalent of a mouse?
The fact that I had never managed to court a woman into
bed. Heterosexual culture was crap, particularly for the
man, I decided. That was one of the things I was rebelling
against.

Into the town centre I swaggered. First, a quick-stop
in a pub to start getting smashed, an essential piece of
the puzzle. Then a shot of sambuca. And then another.
I looked around the pub at the other thirty-somethings.
Lots of couples and mates out with mates from work.
What a boring scene. Fuelled up, I locked in mission
parameters and headed off.

As I walked into Gypsy, I nodded at the doorman, who
recognised me and greeted me with a friendly "How ya
doin', mate?" I went upstairs, and as I hoped, the dance
floor was well populated by fellow gay men. First, a couple
of drinks as I scoped things out.

As I moved, first to the edge of the dance floor, and
then away from the edge, I spotted one of the lads that
I'd danced with last Friday, and he recognised me as I
approached. I, however, screwed my face up with baffle-
ment when I saw him before suddenly exclaiming, "OH,
IT'S YOU AGAIN!" with a manic smile. He laughed, and
his friends, who had caught sight of my flouncing, looked
over. Being funny didn't work against you when you were
gay, it seemed. I started to bust some moves in time to
theirs, and we all began to dance together. Once again, I
was throwing it about, and loving it, and people seemed

to like me all of a sudden. I didn't know how to dance, but I didn't seem to be doing anything wrong. Looking around, my fellow gays had disappeared again. C'est la vie.

At one point, for irony, I decided to give a giggling work group of middle-aged ladies a few thrills when I somehow got sucked into their circle. Clumsily, I stood on the foot of one of the women and quickly apologised.

Damn it, John, a real man wouldn't apologize! Oh, who cares? I'm a gay man now.

I locked eyes with her and mouthed, "Sorry. You okay?" At least being gay meant you could be nice to women. No need to play the cool character now. She nodded that it was fine. To drive the point home, I dropped to my knees and exclaimed, "I'M SO SORRY!" provoking laughs and shakes of the head from her group of friends. She looked amused and embarrassed and indicated for me to stand up. Obviously, she had attracted the attention of a weirdo. Oh, I forgot: women say that they love a sense of humour in a guy who doesn't take himself seriously, but actually, they don't like it.

I was tolerated within their group as I danced. The weirdo that danced with her would form part of a joke on Monday, I bet. In jest, I reached out with my hand to touch her hair, and then jerked it back again, with a look of mock innocence, when she noticed. She shook her head, and then avoided my gaze for a while. Ah well, that's how well I did as a straight man. But I wasn't a straight man now.

I looked her up and down, in a detached way. She looked nice. Pretty. Chubby. About fifty. She would once have been my type. Did she know she was attractive? Living on the floorboards for so long had given me a different perspective. "Every woman has her charms" is the old expression, and to me it had always been true. If I had a type, back when I was straight, I had about a dozen types.

I had made most of my observations on this subject from the comments under porn videos, from bloke-banter down the pub and from looking around at what men actually went for. In my estimation, you could divide men into three groups, in terms of whether they found nearly all female body types attractive. There were people like me who weren't in any doubt about it, and that made up the first third. Second were men who would probably see it my way, if feminists and the rest of society would stop hammering a message into them about what they supposedly liked. The third group were mostly those who just happened to have a very narrow view of what they liked. Good for them, I say. You can't always control what you like. There was a subgroup within that group who just saw women as potential fucktoys to be fucked and nothing else. They were shitheads and you could normally spot them, walking around with their arm around their latest adoring girlfriend.

I used to find most women attractive, even if none of them would give me a second look. I considered leaning over and explaining all of this to the woman. I could tell her that this was objective information and philosophy from a gay man and assure her that she was attractive, as a parting shot. I decided not to bother. Red sambuca was wonderful stuff, but the wisdom it evoked was not always understood by others, I had discovered.

I would try one thing, I decided. I leaned over and bellowed, "I'm gay," and pointed at myself. She was the first person I had told. I wanted to try it on for size, and it felt extremely empowering. She half grinned and half grimaced. Maybe I was a straight guy and this was my chat up line?

I didn't feel like bothering with this stuff any more tonight. Even as a gay man I was getting rejected by women.

Chapter 15

The next month

> "Second star to the right and straight on 'til morning."

New patterns established themselves over the course of the next month. In some ways, the changes were small. For example, at six o'clock one evening, I went for a walk on the beach, even though there was no real need. I got dressed up with some tan chinos and a powder blue shirt. I had learnt that dressing up was worth doing, a little pick-me-up that didn't cost much. Fifteen minutes later, I was at the beach, and I wandered through the crowd as a stranger. A bit of a walk, crouching down to take an occasional photograph of a shell or other leftover bit of sea life, and I had wasted an hour and half not really doing anything. "Keep calm, nothing is under control" was a slogan that I had seen on a poster once. That was the vibe. When I got home, I casually started putting dinner together. Later, as I sat eating it to the accompaniment of some Tom Baker era *Doctor Who*, I remember thinking I had things pretty good.

Keeping a promise to myself, I bought some weights from a local shop and took them home in the car. I set them up immediately but ended up overdoing it. I had a great workout, but the next day I felt so exhausted that I considered calling in sick. By midday, I felt like I was coming down with the flu. By bedtime, I had to hobble up the stairs sideways. I gave it a couple of days before I dared try the weights again but took things slowly second time around. By the end of the first week, I still felt exhausted, but oddly great, too.

During the week, I was thinking about the weekend. My relationship with the dozens of women I bumped into over the course of a week had improved. I was polite and friendly, but no longer their clown. I'd chat to them when I had the chance, but it was a conversation between adults now.

"Oh John, do something to cheer me up!" one of them said in an attempt to initiate the old behaviour. I later gleaned that she had had a falling out with her boyfriend of the moment. In reply, I just smiled without further comment.

I don't think that most of them liked me as much as they used to, but I wasn't bothered. If someone didn't respect me and see me as an adult man, I didn't want to know them. Despite my efforts to amuse and endear myself to them, none of them was a friend, and by that I mean, I had never seen a single one of them outside of work. As for being their jester and their anti-depressant when they were feeling down? I no longer wanted the job.

Things were going pretty good when it came to going out at night. I started off with a big meal to line the stomach; I was planning to get smashed, after all. A nap, if I needed it, followed by a shower before getting dressed up and heading out. Strolling into town, I would find somewhere quiet to get the first drinks in. Once I was sufficiently drunk, I'd usually go to Gypsy or one of the other places I had found. I had made a discovery at a relatively late stage in life: I was a dancer. Is it strange to dance so late? I had decided that, if I can get in enough dancing as possible, everything else seemed to fall into place. As a gay man, I was still trying to have sex, and I didn't have any success to report on that front. But things were different this time around. I was a dancer and a *Doctor Who* fan and a desirer of sex, but the latter didn't define me any more.

My masturbation life had become confusing. I was still mostly looking at straight porn. I reasoned that I had been getting cheap thrills by trying to get a look at heterosexual sexual imagery since I was about twelve years old. Maybe this confusion would always exist? Look at the way cultural ideals of beauty differ. In one society or period of history, fat is beautiful. In another, thin is beautiful. That means that those things are learned. No wonder I was now wired up to be aroused by heterosexual imagery after eighteen years of constant exposure and stimulation. I'd throw in a bit of gay and a bit of bi with the regular stuff to see if I could turn the tide on that one. As it happened, my interest had waned anyway, and I'd gone from at least every other night to about twice a week. For now, I decided, I'd keep using the old stuff and hope that, gradually, a contextual shift would begin to establish itself within me.

Something marvellous happened one morning. I had decided to start jogging on the sea front before work. That sounds admirable, but the real reason for making such an early start was so that I wouldn't be seen. Jesus, I had only been away from this sort of physical activity for a few years and I was a wreck. The first attempt left me gasping for breath after only a few minutes.

Besides, Command had been in contact, damn them. I thought they had forgotten about me. I thought they had given up on me after my last fuck-up, just like I had given up on myself. I had become used to the idea of leading the quiet life of a regular person, in the twenty-first century. I knew what they wanted, the same thing they always wanted: someone (or something) needed rubbing out. This was why I was getting back into shape; I needed to be ready. No doubt, I would soon be up against other, younger agents, also from the future. Or cybernetic androids, I thought, with a wince, remembering a previous assignment, five years ago.

I thought I was alone on the promenade, so I jumped a bit when I heard a male voice say, "Watcher, mate!" It was one of the guys that I'd met a couple of times at Gypsy.

"Hello there," I replied to the man. "Off for a run as well?" I enquired redundantly.

I realised what was about to happen. We were going to fall into conversation and we were going to end up running together. He was about twenty, and while he didn't look like a fitness freak, he didn't look like he would completely embarrass himself. At all costs, up to and including lying about a made-up illness or suddenly pretending to remember an appointment, I felt I must endeavour to avoid this potential humiliation. I hate lying, but mentally, I had dug my heels in over this. Even if I had to fake a sudden heart attack, there was no way I was going to run alongside this fitter, younger gay man.

"Do you want to run together?" he enquired.

"Sure," I replied happily, and off we went.

Having someone else there made me run a better than before. Trying to remain as upright as possible also seemed to help. I was able to keep up for about five full minutes, but after that I had to signal to him to stop.

"Look, the truth is that I've only just started running again. I'm a fat, flabby bastard and I can't keep up," I gasped. Somehow, I found the strength for a Scotty impression and added "I canea teak it anie moor captain!" complete with an impassioned facial expression that made him laugh.

"That's okay," he said with a shake of the head.

Then I remembered, having a sense of humour doesn't equal failure when you're with gay men. I leaned against a wall while we chatted. He asked me if I'd just moved here. I told him that I had lived here my entire life, but that I'd only just started going out at night. I felt that the expression might work as a euphemism that a fellow gay man would understand. It went over without comment. His name was Alan. I remember how he introduced himself: "By the way, my name is Alan." It was polite and direct.

Overall, it was a lovely chat. I wonder why I had presumed that a conversation with a gay man would be about sexual things? I threw in some anecdotes about some of my drunken experiences in the town, which caused mutual laughter. I was still finding my feet in this world, but it seemed that you were allowed to be less than perfect without implying that you were an idiot, unworthy of any respect.

For a younger man, he was reasonably well versed in the geek arts. He wasn't into *Doctor Who*, that was a Russell T. Davies reinforced myth about gay people, but he knew his Bond. He was a Connery man. Interesting. I made a case for Dalton. I put forward my usual thesis that he could have been the best Bond, but he had never been given a great film. You can call me sexist, but I find it difficult to imagine a conversation like that with a woman. Men and women often like different things. If you are in a same-sex relationship, you increase the odds of meeting someone with overlapping interests.

When I felt the conversation had come to a natural end, I said that I was going to limp home.

"No you're not," Alan said, taking me by surprise.

"Right, where I am going?"

"Come on, run to the end with me." He pointed to the end of the seafront.

"I can't," I whined.

"I caaaan't," he mocked. The only camp moment so far.

"Come on," he said before setting off, and I was forced to follow him, out of politeness.

I felt increasingly ridiculous as we progressed along the seafront. It occurred to me that this seemingly nice guy was having a bit of fun at my expense as he effortlessly pounded along. I started to flag, and when he noticed, he said, "Come on!" and increased the pace again. The bastard. There was a point at which I was ready to give in, but "No!" he commanded, and I followed. He sprinted the last bit so that he could turn around to watch me finish. The sod.

"Come on, John!" he shouted from the finish point.

"Sprint finish!"

To show the bastard what I was made of, I did somehow add on some speed for the final fifteen seconds. Fortunately, a bit of the seawall railing came to hand when I gasped over the finish line.

"For fuck's sake!" I exclaimed when I was able.

"Not bad," he opined.

Alan was being a mate. I had struggled to start running again, and when I did, I trundled along like a wet lettuce that didn't want to be in the salad. I needed get out there and push myself a bit, just like everyone did. I had been going through the motions in the least painful way possible.

We said our goodbyes and he headed off at a relaxed pace. I half walked and half jogged home. Physically, I felt awful. And great. I managed another early morning run that week, but thankfully and unfortunately, I didn't see Alan again. What I did do was push myself as hard as I could. What I had thought of as the give up point was actually the pain point, and I could cruise along at that level for most of the run.

By Thursday my face looked thinner, amazingly.

At 10pm, I set off on a quick trip to Tesco. Ironically, although I had the chemicals that everyone else was struggling to obtain, I had run out of jelly.

As usual for that time of night, the car park was half empty. I picked up a trolley, and headed around to the front of the store. As I approached the entrance, I noticed, high up on the wall, a small plastic box with a flashing light on it. No one else was around, so I stopped for a moment to look at it. It must have been something to do with security. I tried an experiment, and sure enough, each time I moved, the little light flashed. Infrared, no doubt. More experimentation proved that I could move a small amount without setting it off. I estimated that I had nearly six metres to go before I reached the covered entrance of the store. Could I make it all the way without setting off the little light?

"Control? It seems like I'm not going to be able to simply walk into the complex after all."

"What are you talking about?"

"Infrared—one scanner about two metres up, on the side of the wall."

"Okay, hang on John. We're bringing up the schematic now. What ever you do, don't move until I find out what it's linked to."

"I'm not going anywhere," I whispered.

A moment later: "Okay, it looks like there's something we missed. The entrance is rigged with an infrared scanner, it's wired into the security system."

"Yes, I know that. I just told you."

"Yes, well there's something you don't know: The complex has four security 'bots just inside the entrance. Walk past them, and they won't do a thing; set of the system, and they'll become active, and then they'll cut you to ribbons."

"Sounds nice. What do I do now?"

Would it have been whining to ask why they didn't check the schematics before I attempted to enter a supposedly unmanned computer complex?

"Our technical people are saying there may be a solution, John. If you can get to the entrance without triggering the system, you should be okay. Those sensors are very basic. Move as slowly as you possibly can. You can—maybe—set the sensor off, once or twice, extremely briefly. It will be interpreted as background noise by the system. There is one bit of good news."

"I'd like to hear it."

"Set off the alarm, and you won't have to time to worry about it."

"Thanks," I said before setting off.

Slowly, I proceeded, shuffling one foot in front of the other. It was painstaking, the empty equipment trolley rattling along the ground. We'd just have to hope that the sensor wasn't keyed for sound too.

"Damn it!"

"What's wrong?"

"I just set off the sensor. I think I got away with it though."

"Stop a minute. There's someone who needs to speak to you."

"Can't it wait?"

"No, it can't wait," said the familiar voice. It was Judi Dench, my boss. "John, we're scrubbing the mission. We had no idea that security was still active around the complex."

"No can do, I'm afraid, Ma'am." She hated it when I called her that. "I'm past the half way point now." That was a lie.

"I don't care. There's no telling what's still active in the complex itself. I'm pulling you out. That's an order."

"Sorry, Ma'am: your transmission is breaking up."

"Damn it, John!"

Slowly, inch by inch, I moved forward. It took me nearly three minutes to cover four metres. Practically out of range of the scanner, I took a risk and rushed towards the automatic door. The world saved, I checked my inside pocket to make sure I had my Tesco Club Card. I was always forgetting that thing.

Everything I did was in service of the weekend. It was my goal, but it was also the test of how well I was doing as a gay man. Working out was knocking me for six and making me feel great at the same time. Apart from the small but noticeable improvement in my appearance, I now felt that I was a work-in-progress rather than something that was gradually going downhill. The changes in my life were like figures in a sum, and hitting the dance floor was the bit between the lines at the bottom, the moment of truth.

I headed out as usual. I had already begun to get to know a new crowd in the clubs and I was on nodding terms with some of the staff. Each time out, step one was to find a quiet corner and start getting a bit drunk. I reasoned that a huge shift in lifestyle would require a bit of assistance. For some, that may be a supportive partner or family, or even working with a councillor. "Go with what works" was my mantra these days, a shot followed by a pint my starting point on an evening out.

As I danced, I surveyed the club. It felt subversive to be having deep thoughts in a place like this. My thinking was muddled due to the alcohol, but as always, direct and clear at the same time. How much closer was I to having a sexual relationship or just simply getting laid? Maybe I was rushing things.

Steady on, John. You're only a few weeks old, in gay terms.

An uncomfortable thought began to form in my mind. How much of this could I have done without the mouse? Don't get me wrong, I had already accepted that a lot of my problems had been my own fault all along. Could I have made the improvements that I had made without going gay? I could have started exercising without the mouse, for example. However, the sequence of events would have been different, and the thought probably wouldn't have occurred to me. The changes I had made were positive, but it was ironic that I hadn't made an improvement in the main area that I had wanted to: my sex life, or my lack of one.

Why had a simple change in sexual orientation brought about such massive changes in other areas of my life? That was a mystery. I concluded that my sexual compass had been drawn in the wrong direction for me in the past. As a heterosexual man, I was a complete failure. I had been forced to play a game that I could never win at. The end result was that I had been trapped in a perpetual losing streak in every part of my life. This month had been instructive, I'd go as far as to say life-changing. Even if I ran out of the ingredients, or if mouse stopped working for some reason, I was determined to preserve the new attitude to life. I was sure that I could do it through willpower alone.

After Gypsy, I stumbled in the direction of Brite House. It was a club that catered to a group I that would have dismissed as teeny-boppers when I was young enough to go there. Maybe, I was secretly jealous at the time. Maybe, I was scared that I wouldn't be good enough. Back then, I would put my Queen album on and shake my head at people who were desperate to be cool.

"Who are you?" exclaimed eighteen-year-old me upon seeing the projection before him.

"I am you," said the ghostly hologram as it shimmered and flickered. "I have used technology that exists in the future to project my image back in time. I am thirty years old now. It is the year 2014."

"What do you want?" my younger self asked.

"I want you to get a haircut and some nice clothes," I replied. "There's a club called Brite House. I want you to go down there and make an effort to get off with someone. At least try."

"Brite House? Get off with someone? I don't understand. Why is that important?"

"Because in the future, you are a miserable, fat, thirty-year-old virgin!" I told me.

"And this… will definitely work?" I asked.

"It is impossible to say, but not making the slightest effort definitely won't work. That is certain. Oh, and start exercising, because you're a right fat bastard in the future." The image spluttered out of existence.

Bang! And then it hit me. The police car, that is.

I'd been wandering around in my fantasy world when I walked into the middle of the road. The car had been travelling slowly and the driver had managed to slam the breaks on in time. I instinctively threw my arms out, touched the front of the car and I was knocked onto the ground. I was too drunk and too stunned to know whether I was injured. I lay there, feeling fairly relaxed when the door of the police car opened.

Oh well, I'm in trouble with the police now. Finally, Stephen can be proud of his brother.

"Are you okay?" the policewoman asked me. Her tone was a mixture of concern and annoyance.

The reality of the situation began to take hold of me. I was not the sort of person who wanted to get into trouble with the police.

Oh, what have I become? The kind of idiot who gets into trouble, that's what. All while drunk, and technically, on drugs. I didn't mean any harm, and there are special circumstances in the form of profound dilemmas and hand-wringing about sexuality. But the end result is the same: Sunday morning, sleeping one off, probably in a police cell.

I started to pull myself together.

Holy shit, I'm going to get into trouble!

New plan: apologise like mad and try to talk myself out of it. I'll assure her that I've never done anything like this before, and that I'm heading straight home.

I started rambling as I got to my feet: "I'm very sorry about that. I wasn't concentrating and I walked out in front of you. To be honest, I've had too much to drunk, I mean drink. I'm not used to it. I am sorry."

"Okay, are you all right?" she asked.

"Yes, as far as I can tell, I'm fine," I replied. I tried to inject a tone into my voice that said, *Let me go, and I'll never do it again. I'm a goody and I don't need a proper punishment when I do something wrong.* It was my simpering version of the Jedi mind trick.

Fortunately, the whole thing happened on a side street; a crowd forming would have complicated things. She must have known what was going on. She must have known she was dealing with a total wimp, who was terrified. She looked around, as though uncertain what to do next.

"Where do you live?" she asked.

I told her my address.

"Get in," she said wearily.

Damn. I was hoping that I could talk my way out of the whole thing. Great, taken home in a police car. Once again, Steven would be so proud. Older brother was finally living up to the younger brother's example. The difference was that it was the result of poor judgement and carelessness in my case. Briefly, I wondered if my twat of a brother would make the same claim about the situations he found himself in. I quickly concluded that yes, he probably would try to claim that, but no, it was generally his own fault when he got into trouble. The other difference was that as this was a woman, she'd end up falling in love with him on the way home. She'd be his girlfriend by the end of next week.

I'll get bollocked for this, and he'd get laid.

She pointed to the passenger side door and I got in as she got back in on the driver's side. Off we went. As we drove along, I tried to sum her up, psychologically. I could still retrieve something from this situation if I was careful. I'd estimate her to be in her mid forties. Did that make me surrogate son material? That was my best shot. Back in the day, I would have found her attractive. No, very attractive. Voluptuous, bouncy body and a pretty face. I could try to feign an interest along those lines, but even when I was straight, chatting up women was my weakest area.

"What a nob head. Are you pissed up?" she enquired.

"I am. It was a mistake. To be honest, I've been going through a tough time recently. A very strange time."

She seemed slightly amused at my earnestness. I still couldn't work out whether I was in life-ruining trouble or not. We arrived at my house.

"Okay, off you go," John.

"Right, so I can just go?"

Idiot. What I just said implied that I might still be in trouble. I should have made it sound like I expected to leave.

"Yes, John. You can go. But don't do that again. You're a nob head. Some of my colleagues would have nicked you for that."

"Thank you," I said, gratefully. "And I won't do it again, I promise."

Yuk. I sounded like I was twelve.

It's just as well that I was out of the heterosexual-with-intent business, because such a display of uncool weakness would have undoubtedly ruined things for me.

"Thanks," I said before quickly letting myself out. I stood on my doorstep and waved at the police car while it departed. I wondered if it was the proper thing to do. I let myself into the house, had a quick pee, and then slept on the couch. As I settled down, I considered the validity of "go with what works". Was it still working?

I was awoken at 8am by a loud knock at the door. It was the policewoman.

I had thought that I had got away with the whole thing, but obviously not.

"Remember me?" she asked.

"I do remember you," I replied, ready to start making more excuses, and wondering why she wasn't in uniform.

It seemed that she had come over to follow up on the incident last night. A sensible person would have said the minimum amount possible, but the exhausting effect of how things were at the moment combined with being hung over loosened my tongue. I told her the whole lot, minus the bit about how I obtained the chemicals. I had the feeling that this story would soon be repeated for the entertainment of the other police officers at the station...
As I raconteured the whole thing to her, she periodically gasped, shook her head or laughed. How the hell was she going to fill the forms in on this one then? At least she wouldn't think I was boring.

"You've not seen the news then?" she enquired with a weary smile.

"News?" I asked.

She fumbled with her iPhone until she found the story she was looking for.

Oh great, I thought to myself on reading the news that mouse was not real and didn't work. Her smile gave me the impression that she had never encountered someone as daft as me before. I had utterly humiliated myself at every turn. A shame, as I would have found her very attractive once. Oh wait, I did find her attractive, I mean. I'm crackers.

Susan's epilogue

Mice Were Not Gay, Says Top Scientist

A scientist from an Edinburgh University has debunked the widely reported story that a group of laboratory mice had exhibited homosexual tendencies when exposed to the chemical insulin. Speaking on BBC Breakfast News this morning, Doctor Alvin Burke told the presenters that the mice had engaged in homosexual behaviour. However, it almost certainly had nothing to do with the insulin-based medications that he and his colleagues had been testing.

"The mice did exhibit homosexual behaviour, which is somewhat unusual in mice," he told them. However, he went on to add that the behaviour quickly dissipated and was never repeated. Subsequently, he and the rest of the team had spent a further month or so attempting to recreate the effect with other subjects without any success whatsoever.

When asked why the laboratory had not retracted its earlier findings, he said this: "We did not retract anything, because we never made a statement to retract." It would seem that the information had been leaked to the press by a junior member of the team who had since been dismissed. When asked why he didn't release a statement to calm the furore, he repeated his earlier point that he had nothing to retract.

Pressed further, he acknowledged that he had been aware of widespread myths that had spread in regard to the effects of insulin on human sexual orientation.

"Yes, I observed the social effects," he said in a tone that he probably normally reserved for a casual aside to one of his lab mice.

I was a twenty-one year old woman, and things were looking up. Mouse wasn't for real, it would seem. It was good that things were back to normal. However, maybe the upheaval had forced people to confront some uncomfortable truths, which was probably for the best too. Comfortable situations are never deadly, by their nature, but they can be utterly stifling. Mouse had given the bottle a damn good shake, long after all of the pieces had been allowed to settle at the bottom.

As for the gay mice, they had the greatest adventure of all. A week after the television appearance by the scientist, after having already inspired, quite possibly, the most notorious sexual scandal in the history of the order Rodentia, they added to their legend by escaping the laboratory. This fuelled the fire within Internet conspiracy mills about the nature of the experiment; the main gist was that mouse had worked and that it was being covered up by the government/huge pharmaceutical corporations/the liberal media elite.

I know what I like to think: The mice initially covered up their newfound sexual awakening when the scientists took an interest in it. That's life; sometimes we have to be enigmatic about our true nature, particularly on matters of sexuality. Once the level of interest had begun to die down, the mice made their plans to escape, possibly taking some insulin with them. It would be nice to think that they found a nice field to live in and be gay together, free from persecution.

I got pleasure thinking about Julie Vinegar-Tits of *The Guardian* finding out what a sham it had all been. Why did I get the impression that she'd soon cook up a theory that made herself look like the victim of yet another male conspiracy? I felt sure that it would be in no way her fault that she'd made an utter fool of herself, as usual.

I wondered how many people had secretly embarked upon private experiments with mouse. Daydreaming again, I imagined someone who had always wanted to embrace his or her sexuality taking some mouse to solidify it and then starting a new life. The darker side was someone who had always desperately tried to fight against their sexual orientation trying mouse and finding it to be a dead end.

Imagine if it had worked. Perhaps it would have become an underground party drug. A dodgy bloke would approach you in a town centre at night and whisper, "Gay night out, love?" You'd then give him a few quid and spend the night, or even the entire weekend, with different sexual orientation.

One morning, while studying, I texted, "fuck off" to Gary. A few minutes later, "fuck you slut" was the reply. That was a bit strong because he *did* call me a slut once. However, his reply kept a grin on my face for the rest of the morning.

When I walked into The Benderland again, it was a relief.

"Oh, and by the way, Rob," I said. "I did think about what you said about my humour being inappropriate. And..." I continued reluctantly as it was hard for me to say it. "I'd like to take that standard lamp over there, stick it up your arse and then switch it on, but then, I think you'd enjoy it too much. About the only action you've had in that region in years." I ended with a huge grin.

"At least you'd be giving *some* pleasure to a man for once," he retorted.

It was nice to be back, but I wasn't going to rely on Gay Club as my one social outlet in the future. Having somewhere dead easy to go to had got me into bad habits, yet another comfortable situation that had to be alleviated. I'd find somewhere else to go, and Gary could come with me.

The one that I couldn't work out was John. Of all the people in my life, he had, oddly, gone through the biggest changes at that time. It could have been a coincidence, or perhaps he had reacted to the stresses of the people around him in some weird way. While the rest of my little world was temporally turned on its side, he had completely reinvented himself. Whatever he had been on, I wished he'd slip me some!

The timing doesn't add up, otherwise, I'd suspect that the new girlfriend had been the cause of the changes. However, that happened after John became supercharged by some force from above. I'd been invited out to meet her one afternoon. She was lovely. She was a lot older than John, but I had a feeling that he was into that. What a great feeling to see someone I care about getting something so good. It was great to think of him exploring the world of sex with someone who presumably had a bit of experience behind her. Her body looked bouncy and rude. She also seemed kind, and I could tell that he appreciated her a great deal. Apparently, along with his mum, I was the main family member that John needed her to meet. She told me this while John was getting the drinks in for us, and a bit of dust must have flown up into my eye or something. In all fairness, I did wonder what would happen when Helen the policewoman met Steven the druggie.

I love that guy, and I should because he is lovable, but if I'm being honest, I found it difficult to respect him until recently. He was the ultimate nice-guy, but he had always shrunk away from being himself. I suppose it was underneath all along. We'd have even more to talk about when he started the degree in September.

What *had* he been getting up to, though? As we were leaving the pub and getting ready to go our separate ways, another slightly chubby middle-aged woman stopped in the street and looked at him with his arm around Helen.

"Not gay now, then, I take it?" she said to him before storming off.

John smirked and claimed ignorance when Helen and I asked who she was and what she was on about.

That weekend, John rang me again.

"Can your parents look after the kid on Saturday?"

"They could, I think. Why, what's up?"

"I want you to come out with me and Helen."

"Erm, where?" I asked while wondering what was going on.

"We're going out clubbing. I want you to come along."

I had to clear my throat because there was more dust in the air, like there had been in the pub.

"Oh right. Are you sure you want me there?" I felt like saying, *Thank you, thank you. I definitely want to come along. I'll be ever so good, and I won't be too sarcastic.*

"Of course. We'll have a laugh. I'll drive, I'm not drinking these days. Helen doesn't like it."

"Okay," I said, as though I hadn't just been thrown a much-needed lifeline. "Oh, can I bring someone?"

"A new boyfriend?" he asked teasingly.

"I wish. I'm going to bring Gary. You don't know him, he's one of Simon's friends. He's not particularly boring, though. He needs a night out as much as I do."

I had a feeling that Simon's curiosity would be piqued in regard to my social endeavours, particularly when Gary communicated stories of hilarious failures in manhunting and the witty accompanying remarks that were made by myself.

A night out. A friend. A sense of hope. Something told me that this was all due to mouse in some way.

The next month

9387913R00081

Printed in Great Britain
by Amazon.co.uk, Ltd.,
Marston Gate.